GRAND CANYON NATIONAL PARK

Tail of the Scorpion

To Lauren + Ryan -- Beware of the scorpion!

Mike Graf

Illustrated by
Marjorie Leggitt

Mike G

FALCON GUIDES

GUILFORD, CONNECTICUT
HELENA, MONTANA
AN IMPRINT OF GLOBE PEQUOT PRESS

FALCONGUIDES®

Text © 2012 Mike Graf
Illustrations © 2012 Marjorie Leggitt

FalconGuides is an imprint of Globe Pequot Press.
Falcon, FalconGuides, and Outfit Your Mind are registered trademarks of Morris Book Publishing, LLC.

Photo credits:
Licensed by Shutterstock.com: title page: © Erik H. Pronske; 5: © Martin Fisher; 6: © Amy Nichole Harris; 7: © Erik H. Pronske; 9: Alexey Stiop; 11 (top): © Erik H. Pronske; 11 (bottom): EuToch; 12: © Brandon Seidel; 16: unknown; 17 © Denis Pepin; 18: © Jason Cheever; 20: © Scott Pehrson; 23 (top): © Paige Falk; 25 (top): Galyna Andrushko; 25 (bottom): © Mark Bonham; 26 (bottom): © Linda Armstrong; 27: © Kevin Lepp; 30–31: © Paige Falk; 32: © Anton Foltin; 33: © Mike Buchheit; 34 (top): © Laurin Rinder; 34 (bottom): © Joel Bauchat Grant; 37: © Rusty Dodson; 41: © Eric Isselée; 45: © Davit Buachidze; 50: © poutnik; 51: © John P. Pearson; 57: N. Frey Photography; 58: © Nelson Sirlin; 62: © James Wibberding; 67 (top): © Paige Falk; 67 (middle): © Shutterstock; 70: © Massimiliano Lamagna; 75: © Erik H. Pronske; 78: © Donald Mallalieu; 83 (middle): © Ferenc Cegledi; 87: © Daniel Korzeniewski; 90–91: © Mikhail A. Shifrin; 96–97: © Khoo Si Lin
Courtesy of National Park Service: 8; 19; 22; 23 (bottom); 26 (top); 42; 63; 67; 71; 79; 83 (top, Mark Lellouch; bottom, Chad Olson)
© Jeff and Paula Hartgraves, www.arizona-vacation-planner.com: 52
Map courtesy of National Park Service

Excerpt from *Brighty of the Grand Canyon* by Marguerite Henry reprinted with permission of Alladin Paperbacks, an imprint of Simon and Schuster Children's Publishing Division. Text copyright 1953 and renewed © 1981 Marguerite Henry.

Illustrations: Marjorie Leggitt
Models for twins: Amanda and Ben Frazier

Project editor: David Legere

Library of Congress Cataloging-in-Publication Data is available on file.

ISBN 978-0-7627-7965-9

Printed in the United States of America

10 9 8 7 6 5 4 3 2 1

"This part is called 'Sunrise,'" Mom said.

"The name sure fits the music," Morgan said.

"I don't know what would be more spectacular in the Grand Canyon," Dad thought out loud, "a sunrise or a sunset."

The music grew louder.

"I can picture the sun lighting up the canyon now!" James, Morgan's twin brother, said.

Morgan called out from the backseat, "I can't wait to get there!"

The family was on a long drive to the Grand Canyon. While on the way, they were listening to the *Grand Canyon Suite*, classical music composed by Ferde Grofé in 1931. The CD switched to track two.

"This part is called the 'Painted Desert,'" Mom said.

"Which is what a lot of Arizona is," James remembered. He pulled out his state road map. "See this area east of the Grand Canyon? This is where the Painted Desert is."

THE PAINTED DESERT

The Painted Desert stretches from southeast of the Grand Canyon to near the New Mexico border. Minerals in the soil make it rainbow colored. Some people call the Painted Desert an area of "badlands" because plants have a hard time growing there. The most famous and picturesque part of the Painted Desert is in eastern Arizona at Petrified Forest National Park.

"Grofé wrote this music for the Grand Canyon?" Morgan asked.

"I remember my teacher telling us that in fifth grade," Mom explained. "Then, when my parents took us there, we listened to the record before we left."

"And we get to hear the CD now!" James exclaimed.

Dad continued driving through the desert. They were still a few hours away from the North Rim of the canyon. While the *Grand Canyon Suite* switched tracks to "On the Trail," James pulled out his journal.

Monday, August 1

This is James Parker reporting.

I'm sure excited about seeing the Grand Canyon! We are driving ten hours in one day just to get there. Mom and Dad say we have to see a Grand Canyon sunset, and hopefully we'll get to see one tonight.

I've been looking at maps of the Grand Canyon for a long time. I can't wait to get an "official" park map. Then I can study all the trails we're going to hike on.

While we're there, we'll spend time sightseeing, learning about the park, and backpacking from rim to rim. That's twenty-one and a half miles of hiking we're going to do in the middle of the desert. That will be awesome! I know I'll have lots to say over the next few days. So expect to hear back from me soon.

Your Grand Canyon Adventurer,

James Parker

Mom took over driving in Fredonia. Soon after, the road started to climb. The hills were covered with pinyon pines and junipers. As they gained more elevation, there were ponderosa pines.

"I guess that's the end of the desert," James said, looking out the window.

"I thought Arizona was all desert," Morgan said.

"The North Rim of the Grand Canyon is more like a mountain than a desert," Dad said. "Its elevation is around 8,000 feet. It is actually very cool and wet most of the year."

"Can you play the 'Sunset' part of the *Grand Canyon Suite* again?" Morgan asked. "That's my favorite part."

"Sure," Mom said.

Listening to "Sunset" gave Morgan a feeling of peace. She pictured the sun gently slipping below the horizon with a huge canyon sprawled out before her. While the music played, Morgan got out her journal.

Monday, August 1
Dear Diary,

I'm listening to music written about a Grand Canyon sunset, and guess what? We're going to get to the Grand Canyon right at sunset, we hope! For James and me it will be our first glimpse of the Grand Canyon. But it's been twenty years since Mom and Dad have been there. They went there together right after they started dating! Dad has been talking about how amazing the Grand Canyon's geology is. Well, he's a geologist, I guess he would know! And Mom says there is an incredible variety of plants and wildlife that live in the park. Since she's a wildlife biologist, I know she's been reading up on the animals there. I can't wait to take pictures of all this with my new digital camera. Dad says it's one of the most photogenic places in the world. I'll write more later!

Yours,
Morgan

The *Grand Canyon Suite* switched to a piece called "Cloudburst." The music started peacefully, and then deep, ominous tones gave the feeling a storm was coming. A strike of a chord sounded like lightning. It was followed by a drumroll of thunder. The orchestra created the sound of howling wind. Then "Cloudburst" burst into a full-blown raging storm.

A giant drop of rain splatted against the car window. And another, and another.

Lightning lit up the sky.

Huge raindrops started pouring down.

Mom turned down the CD. "It looks like we have our own storm to deal with."

"Look at how dark the clouds are!" Dad said.

Morgan pointed toward the forest. "But it's clear way over there."

"It's really coming down now!" James exclaimed.

Mom turned the wipers to full speed just as tiny white balls of ice popped against the car and bounced off the pavement.

"It's hailing!" James called out.

The family drove through the storm. Lightning flashed and thunder rumbled. Rain and hail pounded down. Some of the hail stuck, quickly turning the side of the road into a meadow of white.

They finally reached the park entrance station.

Mom rolled down her window. "It's quite a storm you're having," she said to the ranger.

"Oh, this?" the ranger replied. "It's nothing more than our typical late afternoon summer thunderstorm. It is our monsoon season, you know. This is normal."

"Not where we live," Dad said.

"But as long as we don't get hit by lightning, we like it," Morgan added.

"You're safer in your car," the ranger said. "Here you go." She handed Mom a newspaper and a map of the park. "Enjoy your stay at the Grand Canyon."

"Thanks," Mom said. She rolled up the window and passed the map back to James. Mom slowly drove away from the entrance station.

"It looks like the rain's letting up," James said. He unfolded the map and looked at it.

"And the hail stopped," Morgan added.

Mom turned the wipers down to slow speed.

"And it's clearing up ahead," Dad said. "Hopefully in time for us to catch the sunset."

Mom drove the family toward the Grand Canyon Lodge.

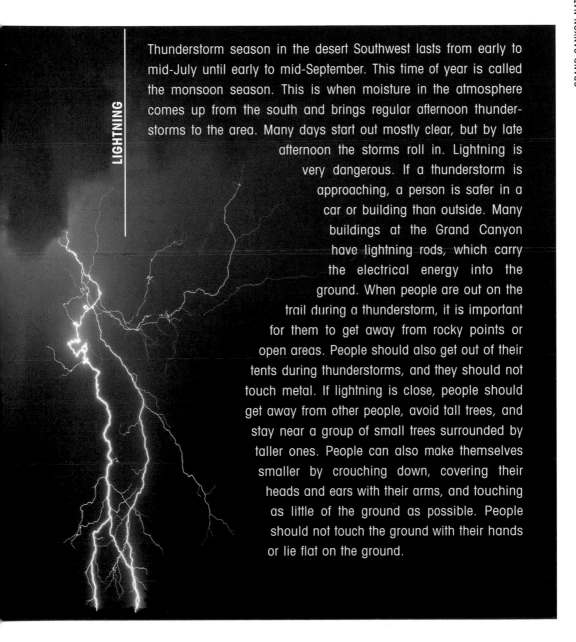

LIGHTNING

Thunderstorm season in the desert Southwest lasts from early to mid-July until early to mid-September. This time of year is called the monsoon season. This is when moisture in the atmosphere comes up from the south and brings regular afternoon thunderstorms to the area. Many days start out mostly clear, but by late afternoon the storms roll in. Lightning is very dangerous. If a thunderstorm is approaching, a person is safer in a car or building than outside. Many buildings at the Grand Canyon have lightning rods, which carry the electrical energy into the ground. When people are out on the trail during a thunderstorm, it is important for them to get away from rocky points or open areas. People should also get out of their tents during thunderstorms, and they should not touch metal. If lightning is close, people should get away from other people, avoid tall trees, and stay near a group of small trees surrounded by taller ones. People can also make themselves smaller by crouching down, covering their heads and ears with their arms, and touching as little of the ground as possible. People should not touch the ground with their hands or lie flat on the ground.

James shut the passenger door. "Hurry up, you guys!"

"Wait. I need to get my sweatshirt," Dad said. He fumbled through the luggage in the trunk.

"Can you get mine too?" Morgan asked. "It's cold out here."

The family was parked near the Grand Canyon Lodge. The storm had stopped, but the parking lot was full of puddles from the rain. A bright orange glow cast over the far western sky. It looked like there was going to be a sunset.

After putting on their sweatshirts, Morgan, James, Mom, and Dad walked quickly through the parking lot toward the lodge.

They walked by an ice machine.

James stopped. "I want to fill up my water bottle."

A couple was in front of him filling their bottles. "We'll miss having ice around in a few days," the man said to the woman.

When the man finished, James stepped up and filled his bottle.

James and his family continued on to the Grand Canyon Lodge. It was a historic building with a sloped roof, massive rock walls, and flat stones on the porches. They entered through heavy doors into a carpeted lobby with giant wooden beams on the ceiling.

"Wow! This is quite a place," Mom said.

Stairs led to a room with a huge rock fireplace, some chairs and couches, and large windows that overlooked the canyon.

They hurried down the stairs. Morgan accidentally bumped into a large metal statue of a burro. "What's that doing here?" she thought, catching up to her family.

Grand Canyon Lodge first opened in June 1928 as a "hotel in the wilderness." The lodge is at the end of the road, and this large log structure dominates visitors' view before they see the canyon. In the lodge's early years, a welcome crew of concession employees greeted visitors by singing. Nightly variety shows were also held there. In 1932, a fire destroyed the first lodge, but it was rebuilt a few years later. Grand Canyon Lodge's gigantic windows face the canyon in the sunroom, where many visitors view the canyon for the first time.

Grand Canyon Lodge has a rustic feel. The park wants to keep it that way. One way they do that is to keep modern technology away. There is no television and limited cell phone service from the North Rim.

"Let's go this way," Mom said. The family scooted out a side door to a large patio.

People were everywhere outside. Some had cameras. Others had binoculars.

"Down here!" Morgan called out. She guided her family to steps leading to an overlook crowded with people.

The family got their first look at the Grand Canyon. They stood quiet and still for a moment gazing at the view.

"It's huge," James exclaimed.

"It's one of the world's largest canyons," Dad said.

"And you can't even see all of it," Mom added.

A few of the canyon's pinnacles and mesas were bathed in fading light. The rest of the canyon was buried in shadows.

"Wait until you see more of the canyon tomorrow," Mom said. "You will be awestruck."

"Wait until we actually cross it," Dad added. "Then you'll see how big it really is."

The sun dipped below the horizon.

The family stood silently and watched, along with the other visitors from all over the world.

As the sun dropped farther, the colors of the sky slowly faded to black.

"I guess we missed it," James said.

"Well, it's not like it will be our only sunset," Mom said. "We'll be here a whole week."

Bundled-up visitors climbed back up the stairs and headed toward the lodge.

"I'm glad we got to see the sunset last night," a man said to a woman beside him.

"What did it look like?" Morgan asked.

"It's really hard to describe," the man said. "But it is incredible."

"You'll just have to see one," the woman said.

"Hey! Didn't we just see you at the ice machine?" James asked.

"Yes, that was us," the woman answered. "We arrived here yesterday, all the way from Minnesota."

"It was a long drive," the man continued, "but, so far, it's been worth every minute."

"He says that now!" the woman said. "I wonder how we'll both feel after we cross the canyon."

"We're not young like you folks," the man went on. "And I don't know how many more miles these legs have left in them."

"We're crossing the canyon too," Morgan said. "Maybe we'll see you on the trail."

"That would be great," the woman said. "I'm Joanna, and this is my husband, Steve."

"This is my mother, Kristen, and my father, Robert," Morgan said.

"It's good to meet both of you," Dad said. "I hope our paths cross again."

Joanna and Steve walked back up to the lodge.

Morgan, James, Mom, and Dad stood a moment longer. At night the canyon was like a giant, mysterious black hole.

"We get to hike out there in two days," James said.

"Except for me," Mom said. "Remember, I'm staying here."

"You sure you don't want to go?" Dad asked.

"Of course I want to go," Mom said. "But I've already signed up for that painting class. That's something I've always wanted to do. Besides, you need someone to pick you up at the end of the trail."

"Sometime between four and eight o'clock on Friday, right?" James asked.

"I'll be there," Mom said. "Just make sure you are."

"We will be," Morgan said. She flicked on her flashlight.

The family followed Morgan up the steps. They walked through the lodge and out to the parking lot. Then they drove to the campground a mile away.

Morgan, James, Mom, and Dad stood at Point Imperial. It was early the next morning.

"Well, if we missed the sunset, at least we got to see the sunrise!" Morgan exclaimed. She snapped some photos of the canyon.

"It's all desert out there, and full of trees up here," James said. "I wonder why."

IT'S NOT A DESERT

The highest elevations at the North Rim of Grand Canyon National Park rise to more than 9,000 feet. The weather is much cooler and wetter in these areas than in the rest of the Grand Canyon. The spruce and fir trees are similar to those found in northern Canada. Deer, mountain lions, coyotes, wild turkeys, and many types of birds also live in these thickly forested areas.

A man rode up on a bicycle. "Oh, sweet sunshine!" he said.

"Wow, you rode all the way out here?" James asked.

"All the way from the campground," the man replied. "I got up early so I could ride without a lot of cars on the road. But it was so much warmer at the campsite. The road out to here was freezing. I felt like I was riding through the Arctic!"

"We saw all the frost," Morgan said.

"Yeah. I thought I was going to get frostbite, my hands were so cold. Well, if you'll excuse me, I'm going to go sit in the warm sun and thaw out. It's been nice chatting with you." The man set his bike by a sunny rock and sat down.

Morgan, James, Mom, and Dad went back to their car. They drove toward Cape Royal.

The road passed through a dense forest until it reached a sign that read GREENLAND LAKE.

They got out of the car. Steam puffed from their mouths with each breath.

"I can't believe how chilly it is," Mom said. "I sure wouldn't want to be out riding my bike now."

They came to a pond surrounded by trees. Morgan took a few pictures of the pond. "It's so different here than in the canyon."

A while later, they stopped at Roosevelt Point and walked along a short trail overlooking the canyon.

"Do you know this point is named after one of our presidents?" James said.

"You're right," Mom said. "I hadn't thought about that."

"I wonder which one?" Morgan said. "There were two President Roosevelts."

"My guess is Teddy Roosevelt," Dad said.

Wild turkey

President Theodore Roosevelt was famous for conserving beautiful places. He first visited the Grand Canyon in 1903. It was then that he said this about the Grand Canyon: "Keep this great wonder of nature as it now is. . . . Leave it as it is. You cannot improve on it; not a bit. The ages have been at work on it, and man can only mar it. What you can do is to keep it for your children, your children's children, and for all who come after you, as one of the great sights which every American, if he can travel at all, should see." On January 11, 1908, Roosevelt designated the Grand Canyon a national monument.

The family got back to their car. Their next stop was a hike out to Cape Final.

They walked two miles through the forest and then came to a group of rocks. James and Morgan scrambled up. Mom and Dad followed.

The views were into the eastern, dry part of the canyon.

"I can see why they call this Cape Final," Dad said. "It feels like we're standing at the edge of the world."

"It is so remote up here," Mom said.

"And beautiful," Morgan added. "How about a group photo?" Morgan placed the camera on a rock. She set the automatic timer and scrambled over to join her family. The camera took a picture of them with the immense canyon in the distance.

"Let's take a look," Morgan said.

Everyone gathered around and looked at the viewing screen on the back of Morgan's camera.

"You know," James said, "I'm really looking forward to hiking across the canyon. Even if it looks so hot."

"I think it's the red rocks and so few plants that make it look like a furnace," Dad said.

"Except along the Colorado River down there," James pointed out.

"It's funny," Mom said. "But somehow when I think of the Colorado, I think of mud and rapids and erosion."

"It sure doesn't look muddy," Morgan said. "It looks green."

To (389)
To (389)

KANAB PLATEAU

KANAB CREEK

KANAB CANYON

Colorado River

GRANITE NARROWS

GRAND CANYON NATIONAL PARK

HUNDRED AND FIFTY MILE CANYON

TUCKUP CANYON

Chikapanagi Point
5889ft
1795m

Great Thumb
Point
6749ft
2057m

GREAT THUMB
MESA

1880ft
573m

Mount Sinyala
5434ft
1658m

FOSSIL
BAY

Stanton Point
6311ft
1924m

TUCKUP
POINT

SB
POINT

MIDDLE GRANITE GORGE

The Dome
5486ft
1672m

• Tuweep

Mooney
Falls

Havasu Falls
Navajo Falls
Supai Falls

HAVASU CANYON

TOROWEAP
VALLEY

Colorado   River

Supai
Fees required.
Not accessible by road.

Apache
Point

Vulcans
Throne
5102ft
1555m

Toroweap Overlook

Havasu Springs

AZTEC
AMPHITHEATER

Lava Falls

Hualapai
Hilltop
5199ft
1585m

Havasu Creek

HAVASUPAI
INDIAN RESERVATION

PROSPECT VALLEY

MOHAWK CANYON

NATIONAL CANYON

AUBREY CLIFFS

HUALAPAI
INDIAN
RESERVATION

COCONINO
PLATEAU

Cataract Creek

To (66)

Unpaved road

Hiking trail

Ranger station

Food service

Picnic area

Gas station

Campground

Lodging

North

0   10 Kilometers
0   10 Miles

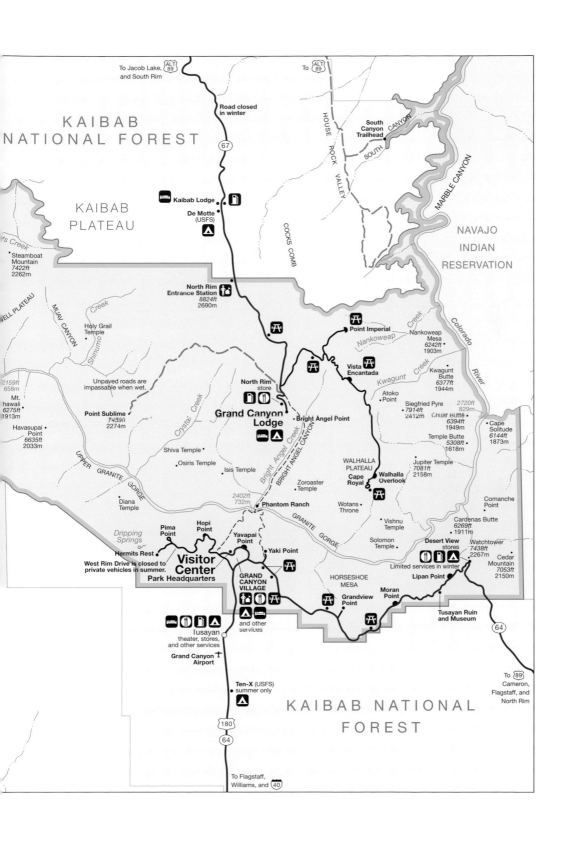

KAIBAB
NATIONAL FOREST

KAIBAB
PLATEAU

To Jacob Lake, ALT 89
and South Rim

Road closed
in winter

67

Kaibab Lodge

De Motte
(USFS)

To ALT 89

HOUSE ROCK VALLEY

SOUTH CANYON

South
Canyon
Trailhead

MARBLE CANYON

NAVAJO
INDIAN
RESERVATION

Steamboat
Mountain
7422ft
2262m

's Creek

WELL PLATEAU

MUAV CANYON

Creek

Holy Grail
Temple

Shinumo Creek

2159ft
658m
Mt.
hawali
6275ft
1913m

Havasupai
Point
6635ft
2033m

UPPER GRANITE GORGE

Point Sublime
7439ft
2274m

Crystal Creek

Shiva Temple

Osiris Temple

Isis Temple

Diana
Temple

Dripping
Springs

Hermits Rest

West Rim Drive is closed to
private vehicles in summer.

Pima
Point

Hopi
Point

Unpaved roads are
impassable when wet.

North Rim
Entrance Station
8824ft
2690m

Point Imperial

Nankoweap Creek

Nankoweap
Mesa
6242ft
1903m

Colorado River

Vista
Encantada

Kwagunt Creek

Atoko
Point

Kwagunt
Butte
6377ft
1944m

North Rim
store

Grand Canyon
Lodge

Bright Angel Creek

Bright Angel Point

BRIGHT ANGEL CANYON

Zoroaster
Temple

WALHALLA
PLATEAU

Cape
Royal

Walhalla
Overlook

Siegfried Pyre
7914ft
2412m

2720ft
829m

Chuar Butte
6394ft
1949m

Temple Butte
5308ft
1618m

Jupiter Temple
7081ft
2158m

Cape
Solitude
6144ft
1873m

2402ft
732m

Phantom Ranch

GRANITE GORGE

Wotans
Throne

Vishnu
Temple

Solomon
Temple

Comanche
Point

Cardenas Butte
6269ft
1911m

Watchtower
7438ft
2267m

Cedar
Mountain
7053ft
2150m

Desert View
stores

Limited services in winter

Lipan Point

Yavapai
Point

Yaki Point

Visitor
Center
Park Headquarters

GRAND
CANYON
VILLAGE

and other
services

HORSESHOE
MESA

Grandview
Point

Moran
Point

Tusayan Ruin
and Museum

64

Tusayan
theater, stores,
and other services

Grand Canyon
Airport

Ten-X (USFS)
summer only

180

64

To Flagstaff,
Williams, and 40

KAIBAB NATIONAL
FOREST

To 89
Cameron,
Flagstaff, and
North Rim

They finally reached the end of the road at Cape Royal. They started walking on a short trail around the cape.

"Look at that hole in the rock," Morgan said. "It's right below the lookout."

"That must be Angel's Window," James said.

Mom, Dad, Morgan, and James walked out to a jutting rock above the hole. It had protective railings along the sides.

"That's quite a drop," James commented while looking straight down.

The family stood at the overlook for a few minutes admiring the view. "You know what sounds good?" Morgan said.

"What?" Mom asked.

"Lunch back at those picnic tables near our car," Morgan replied.

"That's a great idea," Mom said.

They finished the walk around Cape Royal and headed back to the car for the food.

While the family was eating, the bike rider from earlier that day rode up. He took off his helmet and wiped the sweat off his brow.

"Hey, you made it!" Dad exclaimed.

"Yeah. It wasn't easy," the man said. "And it's not a great road for riding. There's a lot of traffic. But the views along the way are incredible."

"I bet you're glad it's warmer," James said.

"Yes," the man replied. "All I've been thinking about for the last ten miles is filling my water bottles at that ice machine at the lodge. But I guess that's the Grand Canyon—a place of extremes."

Angel's Window

"We're going to hike across the canyon starting tomorrow," James said.

"Lucky you," the man answered. "I suppose there are many ways to see this great place. Maybe your way is the best."

"Ask us that when we're done," Dad joked.

The bike rider laughed, and then he headed off.

Dad signed the form for the camping permit at the backcountry office. He attached the permit to his pack.

"Thanks for your help," he said.

"Good luck," the ranger said. "I've hiked across the canyon many times. I know you will really enjoy it."

The shuttle van drove up outside the office.

"Our ride's here," James called out.

"Well, I guess this is it," Dad said.

They stepped outside and met the driver. He helped them put their backpacks in the back of the van.

"Enjoy your class," James said to Mom as he, Morgan, and Dad climbed into the van.

The van headed off on a five-hour drive to the South Rim, where Morgan, James, and Dad would start their hike later that day.

After a while, the van drove out of the park. It passed through the Navajo Indian Reservation. The land was sparse and made up of hills and mesas.

"It doesn't rain much out here, does it?" Dad asked.

"Nope," the driver said, "just like most of Arizona."

They drove on. James, Morgan, and Dad stared out the windows of the van and watched the scenery go by. Outside, the sun blazed down on the Arizona desert. It was just morning, but they passed a man sitting in the shade. He wiped the sweat off his forehead as they drove by.

"It looks hot out there," James said. He took a sip of his water.

"And the day is just starting," the driver replied. "It's supposed to get up to 110 degrees down at Phantom Ranch today."

"We're going to miss this air conditioning," Dad said.

The Grand Canyon has three different zones: the North Rim, the South Rim, and the Inner Canyon. The North Rim is the highest in elevation. It's covered in forest and gets the most precipitation. It is the coolest part of the canyon. The average summer temperatures are a high of seventy-seven degrees Fahrenheit and a low of forty-six. The South Rim is a mix of high desert and forest. The average summer temperatures there are eighty-four and fifty-four. The Inner Canyon is a hot, dry desert, and its average summer temperatures are 106 and seventy-eight.

IN THE ZONE

They came to the town of Cameron. The driver turned west on Highway 64. The road started climbing. They passed several Native American jewelry stands along the side of the road. Higher up there were views of deep canyons. Pinyon pine trees and junipers dotted the hills.

"We're getting close," Dad said.

After a while, they entered the Kaibab National Forest. They were higher up on a plateau. There were many small trees and shrubs, but it still looked dry.

The bus driver pulled up to the park entrance station for the South Rim of the Grand Canyon. Dad showed his park pass and they drove into the park.

After turning a few more bends in the road, the driver pulled into a parking lot. "See that tower?" The driver pointed. "If you get a chance, I really recommend climbing up there. It was built to model Ancestral Puebloan towers once found in Arizona, New Mexico, Utah, and Colorado. It's also an incredible place, and the views of the canyon are worth every step up the spiral stairs."

The driver drove out of the parking lot and back onto the main road. "Get ready for the view of your lives," he announced.

Morgan, James, and Dad sat up with anticipation.

The driver turned another corner. Suddenly views of Grand Canyon were spread out before them.

"It doesn't look real," Morgan said.

"Kind of like a painting," James added.

After passing several more viewpoints, the driver pulled up to Grand Canyon Village. He stopped near the Bright Angel trailhead. Morgan, James, and Dad unloaded their packs from the van.

"Thanks for everything," James said.

"You're most welcome," the driver replied.

Morgan, James, and Dad walked over to a railing and gazed out at the canyon. It was a maze of buttes, mesas, cliffs, and colored layers of rocks. Far below, a trail wove its way toward a small grove of trees. In the distance lay the forested North Rim. Above the canyon, the sky was deep blue and dotted with small, puffy clouds.

"The view of a lifetime," Dad commented.

Morgan looked at the trail. "There are people way down there!"

RIM VISITORS

The South Rim gets about 90 percent of the Grand Canyon's visitors and is open all year. It has lodges, restaurants, gift shops, and stores. The South Rim also has many views of the canyon and trails leading along and into it. There is a free shuttle bus service in the Grand Canyon Village area for visitors.

The North Rim is quieter and more rustic and remote. It is usually closed each year from October through May due to snow.

James pulled out his map. "I think that's the Bright Angel Trail. But we're going down a different trail."

"Why aren't we taking that one?" Morgan asked.

"The trail we're going on is shorter," Dad answered, "so we can get all the way to the bottom of the canyon by tonight."

Morgan, James, and Dad stared into the canyon for a few more minutes.

"It is one huge hole in the ground," Dad concluded.

Morgan held up her camera. "I almost forgot: pictures!" She took several shots of the canyon.

"Come on," Dad said. "Let's take a little walk so we can at least see a few things around here before we head down. It's one o'clock now, and we should be on the trail by three. That way, we'll miss hiking during the hottest part of the day."

THE MOST SCENIC

The Grand Canyon is 277 miles long. From the South Rim to the Colorado River, it is about one mile deep. At Grand Canyon Village, it is ten miles across to the North Rim. It is not the deepest canyon in the world, but it is considered to be the most scenic. It was made into a national park in 1919 and now gets about five million visitors a year.

They started walking on a path along the rim.

Right next to the trail were art studios, lodges, and gift shops. And beyond that were views into the canyon.

Morgan, James, and Dad stopped and got some ice cream. They sat on a bench overlooking the canyon.

"Nice, cool ice cream!" James said. "Thanks, Dad."

"You're welcome," Dad said. "Are you ready for the big hike?"

"Yes," Morgan and James answered.

They hopped on a South Rim shuttle bus and took off their backpacks.

The bus driver dropped them off at the South Kaibab trailhead. They unloaded their packs and walked to a drinking faucet. James, Morgan, and Dad each took a long

Ooh-Aah Point

drink of water and filled up their water bottles. James drank some more from the faucet.

"Leave some for the fish," Morgan joked. But then she too drank more water.

They got to the trailhead right at three o'clock.

Morgan got out her camera. "Stand there," she said, pointing to the sign at the trailhead. She set the auto timer on the camera and ran over to join James and Dad.

The camera clicked.

Morgan, James, and Dad put on their packs and took their first steps into the Grand Canyon.

The trail was cut into the side of a steep cliff that dropped far into the canyon. Morgan, James, and Dad hiked

down one switchback after another.

"I sure wouldn't want to be hiking up this trail," James said. "It's so steep."

"And there's no water," Dad added.

"Are you nervous?" James asked.

"Who, me?" Dad answered. He glanced back up to the top of the rim. "Well, maybe a little bit. But it's too late now."

"Don't worry, Dad," Morgan said, "we'll take care of you."

Dad smiled. "And I'll take care of you too."

South Kaibab Trail

They hiked on. At times, the three- to four-foot-wide trail was covered in loose dirt and rocks. At other times, steps were built into the trail to help with the footing.

They soon came upon some hikers coming up the trail.

The hikers stopped in the shade. "Hi!" one of them said, breathing heavily.

"How far did you go today?" Morgan asked.

"Just to Cedar Ridge," one of the hikers answered. "We figured that was going to be a hard enough climb out. And we were right." He wiped the sweat from his brow and then bent over and took a deep breath.

"Are you all right?" Dad asked.

"Yes, I think so," the man said. "I'm just not used to this heat, I guess."

"Maybe it's the elevation too," a person in the group suggested. "We're almost at 7,000 feet."

The man grabbed his water bottle and sat down. "Let's take a break here," he said to the other hikers.

MORE THAN A DAY

Grand Canyon hikers should not attempt to hike down to the river and back in one day. While hiking down may seem easy, hiking up can be extremely difficult. It is seven miles and 4,780 feet of climbing from Phantom Ranch to the top of the South Kaibab Trail, with no water available along the way.

Hikers should make sure they have enough food, water, and sun protection. Hikers should also avoid hiking in the middle of the day, when it's usually the hottest.

Morgan, James, and Dad took gulps of water from their water bottles and hiked on.

The trail came to a rocky point that overlooked the whole canyon.

James looked at the map he got from the permit office. "I think this is Ooh-Ahh Point."

"Ooh! Look at that view," Morgan said.

"Ahh! I get to stop and rest my feet," Dad added.

Morgan laughed then set down her pack and got out her camera. "You can see so much of the canyon from here."

While Morgan looked for the best picture, Dad and James sat and drank water. They saw a hiker walking briskly up the trail.

"She's going faster uphill than we were going downhill," James said.

A few minutes later, the hiker approached them. "Hi!" she said. She wore a gray and green uniform. A National Park Service pack was slung on her back. "Is everything okay?"

"Yes," Dad answered. "You look like you've done this trail before."

The hiker smiled. "I'm on the trail crew for the summer. Part of my job is to hike down to Cedar Ridge to clean the bathrooms."

"Hey! Can you take our picture?" Morgan asked.

"Of course," the woman replied.

Morgan, James, and Dad propped up their packs and stood next to each other.

"You've got the whole canyon in the background," the woman said. "It will be a great picture. Smile, everyone." The woman snapped the picture and then handed the camera back to Morgan.

"Well, I've got to go. Good luck!" the woman called out, striding up the trail.

"I hope we're as fast as she is when we hike out of the canyon," James commented.

"She does this all the time," Dad said. "No wonder she makes it look so easy." He pulled out his sunscreen and put some on his arms, neck, and face. Then he passed the sunscreen to Morgan and James. They looked out at the canyon ahead of them.

"It looks like the moon," James said. "There are hardly any plants."

They put their packs back on and continued hiking. Soon they met a string of mules heading out of the canyon. James, Dad, and Morgan stepped to the inside of the trail.

The guide riding the mule in front nodded his head as the mule trudged by.

RULES OF THE ROAD

Mules have the right-of-way in the canyon. When approaching a string of mules, hikers should follow the instructions of the guides and stay on the uphill side of the trail, away from the cliff.

"Hello," James, Morgan, and Dad said.

The string of mules tramped by.

When the last mule passed, Morgan stepped back on the trail. "Did you see how the mules were sweating?" she asked.

"It was dripping down their faces!" Dad said.

"That's going to be us pretty soon," James said. He hopped off a small rock and back onto the trail. A large lizard scampered out from under the rock.

"Hey, look at that!" Dad called out.

The lizard dashed toward the side of the trail and paused.

Morgan, James, and Dad watched the lizard. It moved its body up and down.

"It looks like it's doing push-ups," Morgan said.

"It's so big!" James said. "And look at that yellowish green ring around its neck."

"I think it's a collared lizard," Dad said. "It's beautiful, isn't it?"

James took a step toward the lizard, but it scampered into a crack between some rocks.

James walked back toward the middle of the trail. "I guess we better watch where we step," he concluded.

Collared lizard

Morgan, James, and Dad continued hiking down.

Soon, they came to Cedar Ridge, a resting point one and a half miles from the rim.

They spent a few minutes there nibbling on snacks and drinking water. The thermometer posted in the sun by the bathrooms read 104 degrees.

Farther down the trail they came to the Tonto Trail junction, a faint path in the Inner Canyon.

"I'm sure glad we're not going that way," Morgan said.

"Me too," Dad agreed after gulping down water. "That trail looks like it leads to the middle of nowhere."

James and Morgan got out their water bottles. It was still hot, with a dry, biting wind.

Dad scanned the canyon and horizon with his binoculars. Morgan and James each took turns looking through them.

Morgan saw a bird flying in circles high in the sky. "That bird seems so big!" Morgan exclaimed. "I wonder what kind it is."

Dad looked up at the bird. "I've read that condors were released in northern Arizona, not too far from the Grand Canyon. They're the largest flying bird in North America."

"Can I see?" James asked.

Morgan gave James the binoculars. He found the bird and followed it. "It's so far away," he said. "It's hard to tell how big it is."

Morgan, James, and Dad put their packs back on and shuffled down the steep switchbacks.

They came to an abandoned backpack lying next to the trail.

Morgan, James, and Dad stopped to look around for people, but they saw no one.

"That's strange," Dad said.

They turned a bend in the trail and found another backpack. This one was flat on the ground with its shoulder straps facing up. Several of its pouches were unzipped.

James stopped and called out, "Is anyone out there?"

The only sound they heard was the whistling of the hot, dry wind blowing up from the canyon.

"Hello up there!" Morgan shouted. Then she looked down the trail. "Hello down there!"

"Is everyone okay?" Dad yelled.

There was no answer.

"Maybe it's the trail crew," Morgan said.

"It could be," Dad said. "But there's no sign of a camp anywhere. Besides, there's no water in this area, so why would anyone leave their packs here?"

They hiked on and came to an overhanging rock. James, Morgan, and Dad stepped onto the rock and looked down.

"There's the Colorado River!" James exclaimed. "Phantom Ranch must be up that way." He pointed toward a side canyon lined with trees. It had a creek running through it.

"Look," Morgan said, pointing to the trail a few switchbacks below them, "there are two hikers down there without packs on!"

Morgan, James, and Dad watched the two hikers. They sat down on a rock for a minute. The man bent forward and rubbed his head. The lady leaned back and took a deep breath. Then they got back up and slowly continued down the trail.

Morgan, James, and Dad picked up their pace. As they did, they closed in on the two hikers. The man leaned heavily on his walking stick with each step. The woman stopped and put her hands on the rock wall to brace herself.

Morgan caught up to them. "Are you two okay?" she asked.

The couple stopped. The woman slowly turned to face Morgan, James, and Dad. She looked dazed, and her eyes were glassy.

"Not really," the woman answered. "We ran out of water several miles ago, and . . ."

"Hey, it's Steve and Joanna!" James said.

"Do . . . we . . . know . . . you?" the man asked in a raspy voice.

Dad held out a water bottle. "Here, have some."

Steve leaned back on a rock and took a deep breath. "No thanks. You need it."

"Take as much water as you want," Dad said. "Really."

"Are you sure?" Steve asked.

"We've got plenty." Dad looked at James and Morgan.

Steve took a long gulp of water, stopped, and then took another. "Whew!" he said. "I was really losing it there." He took out some crackers and started nibbling.

"Now it's your turn," Morgan said, giving her bottle to Joanna.

Steve handed Joanna some crackers. "Here, honey, you better eat too."

"We saw a couple of packs up there," James said. "Are they yours?"

"We couldn't carry them anymore. The weight in this heat was just too much," Joanna answered. "Now I remember you. We met you at the North Rim at sunset a few nights ago."

"Why didn't we see you on the shuttle over here?" James asked.

"You must have taken the van to the South Rim," Joanna said. "We're doing the opposite. We drove our car over here and will return in the van to get to our car. Didn't you have someone else in your group?"

"Our mom stayed behind," Morgan explained. "She is picking us up at the trailhead on Friday."

"Hmm," Dad thought aloud, "do you think you can you make it down to Phantom Ranch?"

"We hope so," Joanna answered, "but it will be slow going."

"Do you need any food?" Morgan asked.

There are several heat-related issues that can happen to hikers in the canyon.

1. **Heat exhaustion.** This is caused by dehydration from over-sweating. Victims who have this may look pale, feel nauseous, have cool, moist skin, and suffer from cramps. Hikers with heat exhaustion need to drink water, eat high-energy foods, rest, and cool down.

2. **Hyponatremia.** Hyponatremia has similar symptoms to heat exhaustion. It is caused by a low amount of sodium in the blood. It can happen by drinking too much water, not eating salty snacks, and losing electrolytes through sweat. Victims may be nauseous, vomit, and urinate often. They need salty foods and possibly emergency help. Their mental state needs to be watched.

3. **Heatstroke.** Heatstroke is very dangerous and can be fatal. The body's cooling system no longer works. Two to three cases occur each year at the Grand Canyon. People with heatstroke have a flushed face, dry skin, weak or rapid heartbeat, high body temperature, and poor judgment, and they may be unconscious. Victims need shade, to be cooled down with water, and emergency help.

It is possible that in extreme or near-death cases, heat issues can affect people's minds and they can hallucinate.

"No thanks," Steve said. "We took some with us. And we can buy food down there anyway."

"But how will you camp?" James asked.

"We haven't thought that far ahead yet," Joanna answered. "Right now we just want to get there."

Dad looked back up the trail. "I've got an idea."

Dad explained his plan. Then Morgan, James, and Dad pulled off their packs. They left the packs with Steve and Joanna and climbed back up the trail.

They found Steve and Joanna's packs. Dad slipped one on. Morgan and James held the other between them. They walked back down.

Steve and Joanna were sitting on a rock waiting.

"You two look better already," Dad said to them.

"We really don't know how to thank you," Steve said.

"We're glad to help," Morgan answered.

Morgan, James, and Dad put on their own packs.

Colorado River at its confluence with Bright Angel Creek

Joanna suddenly stood up and looked at Steve. "Why don't we give it a try too?"

"Okay. Good idea," Steve said while standing up.

"It's not much farther," James encouraged.

Steve and Joanna slowly put their packs back on.

Morgan, James, and Dad watched Steve and Joanna start down the trail.

"I think they're going to make it," James said.

Morgan, James, and Dad followed Steve and Joanna. The five of them slowly headed toward Phantom Ranch.

Archaeological site in the Grand Canyon

Farther down the trail, they walked through a long tunnel carved into a rocky hillside. After the tunnel, they stepped onto a metal footbridge that crossed over the wide Colorado River.

They stopped in the middle of the bridge and looked down at the clear, flowing water. "We've made it to the bottom of the canyon!" Dad announced.

"We've come down almost 5,000 feet," James said.

"Incredible!" Dad said.

"We wouldn't have made it without you," Joanna said.

They crossed the bridge and turned toward Phantom Ranch. Along the way, they passed the remnants of an old stone structure.

"This looks like an Ancestral Puebloan home," Joanna said.

"You mean Native Americans built this?" Morgan asked.

"This and many other things in the canyon," Joanna answered.

The Colorado River now runs clear and cool—not much more than forty-six degrees year-round. That's the water's temperature when it is released from Glen Canyon Dam 200 feet below Lake Powell's surface. Before the dam was built, the Colorado River was often brown and muddy. The water temperature ranged from near freezing in winter to almost eighty degrees in summer. The constant water temperature and controlled release from below the dam has changed the Colorado River's ecosystem. Some plants and animals have almost disappeared, such as a fish called the humpback chub, which is an endangered species in the canyon. Several organizations are trying to restore the natural ecosystem and bring back the beaches along the Colorado River. To do this, they have purposely released extra water in the canyon several times. This has brought some of the muddy sediment back from the bottom of the river into the flow so it can be deposited as sand and dirt along the banks.

Humpback chub

Several structures are along the Colorado River near the junction of the South Kaibab Trail and Bright Angel Creek. The structures are ancient stone houses. Trails, pottery, and other artifacts have been found nearby. The Ancestral Puebloan people built these houses. They farmed and hunted in the canyon between AD 1100 and 1140. Around 1150, they left the Phantom Ranch area, possibly because of a long drought.

Archaeologists have recorded more than 4,000 archaeological sites in the Grand Canyon National Park area. The sites include structures, pottery, flakes, arrowheads, pictographs and petroglyphs, granaries, and old irrigation dams. The oldest sites date back 10,000 years. But only a very small part of the canyon has been surveyed. New sites are discovered all the time. If visitors come upon archaeological remains, they should leave them alone and report the sites to the National Park Service.

Farther up the trail, Morgan, James, Dad, Steve, and Joanna came to a restroom with lush plants around it. It also had a water fountain outside. They guzzled down some cool, fresh water.

"I feel so much better!" Steve said.

They filled up their water bottles and headed toward camp.

Morgan, James, and Dad found an empty campsite next to the creek.

Steve and Joanna set up their camp a few sites away.

Hikers were wading in the cool water of the stream. Morgan and James looked at Dad. "I know what you are thinking!" Dad said.

They put their packs on the picnic table and walked down to the creek. James, Morgan, and Dad took off their shoes and stepped into the water. Dad sat down right in the stream. "Ahh," he said, "I needed this!"

James and Morgan joined Dad. They sat in the gurgling creek and cooled off.

"This is the best way to end a hike like that," Morgan said.

"Absolutely," Dad agreed. "Look at how many people are in the water." He splashed water all over his face and arms.

James dunked his head under the water. "It's not quite a shower," he said, "but I'll take it."

By the time they got out of the creek, it was starting to get dark. Morgan, James, and Dad worked quickly to put up their tent and organize their supplies.

Morgan got out their small backpacking stove. James got food out of his pack for dinner. Dad found the matches.

James plopped down on the bench. "It's too hot to cook."

Dad looked at a box of dried curry. "You might be right. How about you, Morgan? Are you hungry?"

"I don't feel like having anything hot either," Morgan answered. "We could just eat cheese and crackers and dried fruit."

"I bet Mom's putting together quite a camp dinner right now," James said.

"Or perhaps she's eating at the lodge restaurant," Dad said.

"And looking out the windows, wondering where we are," Morgan added.

While Morgan, James, and Dad ate, people kept walking past their campsite.

"Where's everyone going?" James asked.

"To the campfire program," a person answered.

Morgan, James, and Dad looked at each other. They hurried to finish their food.

After eating, they put all their food into a stuff sack and hung it, along with their backpacks, on the tall metal poles at their campsite.

"Hopefully that will be high enough off the ground to keep the critters out," Dad said.

James zipped up the tent.

They walked over to Steve and Joanna.

"We're going to the campfire program," James said. "Do you want to join us?"

Steve and Joanna looked at each other. "I think we've had enough excitement for the day," Joanna said. "But thanks for asking. Will you tell us about it tomorrow?"

"Of course," Morgan replied.

By the time Morgan, James, and Dad got there, the talk was already going on. They sat down in the back.

A ranger pointed to the South Rim far above them. "Look up there," she said. "Do you see those flashes? Those are from people taking pictures of the sunset at Mather Point. Okay, everyone, smile and wave!"

The people in the audience laughed while waving their arms.

"There's no way they'd see us all the way down here," James said.

"Maybe if they have a telephoto lens," Morgan said.

"You know," the ranger said, "for being in the middle of the wilderness, there's a lot of nightlife going on around here. Would you like to know where all the action is?"

Several people in the audience nodded their heads.

"The main attractions I want to tell you about aren't human," the ranger began.

Gray fox

Morgan and James looked at each other.

"Many of the Grand Canyon's animals only come out at night," the ranger explained. "They are nocturnal. It's hard to blame them. The temperature reached 114 in the shade here today. And the humidity was only 5 percent. That's so dry that some streams in the Inner Canyon stop flowing during the daytime! Down here at Phantom, the ringtail cat, the gray fox, the great horned owl, and the spotted skunk are fairly common. And they are all out and about once the sun goes down."

"I hope we don't see a skunk in camp," James said to Dad and Morgan.

"And there are nineteen species of bats that live at the Grand Canyon," the ranger continued. "But the creature I want to tell you about the most is just two inches long." The ranger held out her thumb and finger a couple of inches apart. "Does anyone have an idea what I'm talking about?"

"Scorpions?" Morgan guessed.

"That's right," the ranger responded. "The Grand Canyon has two species. The desert hairy scorpion, which can grow to six inches, and the bark scorpion, which is two inches long and is much more venomous. During the day, they rest under rocks, in crevices, and in burrows. But at night, it's a whole different story."

"I hope we don't run into one of those!" Dad said.

OLDER THAN DINOSAURS

Scorpions are arachnids and have lived on Earth for more than 400 million years—since long before the dinosaurs. There are more than 1,500 different species of scorpions worldwide.

Scorpions give birth to large litters. Their live young climb onto the mother's back until they can hunt for themselves. Scorpions can live up to twenty-five years.

Scorpions eat insects and small rodents. A scorpion paralyzes its prey by using the stinger on the tip of its tail. About twenty-five species of scorpions can kill a person, including Grand Canyon's bark scorpion, although deaths from scorpion stings are extremely rare.

"Many Phantom Ranch rangers have been stung over the years, some of us more than once," the ranger explained. "But that's the risk we take for getting to work here at Phantom. And, by the way, we had two people stung in camp last night."

Morgan looked at Dad, then James. "Good thing we zipped up our tent!" she said.

"By now you're all probably wondering where these scorpions are," the ranger continued. "Let me show you!"

James sat forward. Dad looked at Morgan and James.

The ranger held up a special flashlight. "At night you can see the scorpions easily with ultraviolet light." The ranger stepped into the audience and handed out flashlights. Morgan took one.

"Follow me," the ranger called out.

The campers followed the ranger. They shone their lights into the grass and bushes next to the trail.

"Here's one!" someone yelled.

Morgan, James, and Dad hurried over to look. Under the light was a small, glowing insect. It had two claws on the front of its body. Its tail curled up over its back.

"Eeew!" Dad said.

"I sure wouldn't want to have one of those crawling on me!" James exclaimed.

Morgan walked on. James and Dad followed her. She shone her light on the other side of the trail. Within a moment, Morgan saw something glowing in the grass. She moved her light closer and found another tiny scorpion.

While the family watched the scorpion, the ranger walked up. "Try looking at it with a regular flashlight," she suggested.

Morgan turned off her ultraviolet flashlight. She pulled her regular one from her pocket and shone it on the scorpion. This time, they couldn't see it.

"Okay," the ranger said, "turn on the ultraviolet light again."

Morgan flicked on the special flashlight. The scorpion was still there.

"It's completely translucent," the ranger explained.

"Why do they glow like that?" Morgan asked.

"Good question," the ranger replied. "Scorpions have a chemical in their body that glows, or fluoresces, even after they die. The only time they don't glow is when they shed their outer layer and haven't grown a new layer yet."

"There's one over here!" someone called out. The ranger headed over to see it.

James, Morgan, and Dad found several more scorpions within a few feet of the trail.

"Boy," Dad said, "they're everywhere."

"And without the ranger's flashlight, we wouldn't even know it," James added.

They reached the ranger, who was waiting at the end of the trail. "How many did you see?" she asked.

"Eleven," James replied.

"They're sure active tonight," the ranger said.

Great horned owl

Phantom Ranch has been described as "a little bit of civilization in the wilderness." It is located near the junction of Bright Angel Creek and the Colorado River at the bottom of the Grand Canyon. The ranch has stone and wood cabins, dormitories, and a dining hall. You can only get there by foot, mule, or raft.

Before the ranch was constructed, David Rust built a small campsite there in 1902. It was called Rust's Camp. Theodore Roosevelt camped at Phantom Ranch in 1913, and it was renamed Roosevelt's Camp that same year.

In 1922, Mary Jane Colter, an architect, designed Phantom Ranch. Construction began that year, and the ranch was completed ten years later. Colter named the place Phantom Ranch after Phantom Creek, which runs into the canyon one mile up from the Colorado River. During the Great Depression, the Civilian Conservation Corps (CCC) set up camp where the Bright Angel Campground is today. The CCC built a swimming pool. But because of overuse and floods that caused bacteria to form in the water, in 1972 it was filled in.

Electricity was installed at Phantom Ranch in 1966. Modern sewage treatment was added in 1981. Phantom Ranch is now a popular tourist destination. Reservations are required long in advance to stay there.

"That's more than I want to know about," Dad said.

Morgan handed the ultraviolet flashlight to the ranger.

"Just remember," the ranger reminded them, "stay on the trail and out of the bushes. And don't go anywhere barefoot."

"Got it," Dad said.

James, Morgan, and Dad headed toward camp. They shone their flashlights back and forth on the trail.

"We might not see the scorpions without the ultraviolet light," James said.

"But at least we can see where the trail is," Morgan observed.

Dad grabbed Morgan and James's arms. "I've got an idea. Let's go to the canteen and get something cool to drink before we call it a night. I'm not sure I want to be in camp right now anyway."

"Good idea," James said.

They turned and walked back toward Phantom Ranch.

They got to the canteen and went inside. The room had benches and large tables. Ceiling fans spun slowly. Hikers were hanging out, reading, talking, and playing board games.

Morgan, James, and Dad ordered lemonade. The twins found a game of checkers.

"I'm glad that couple from Minnesota finally made it into camp," a person nearby said. "They sure looked tired."

Dad turned to the people who spoke. "We saw them on the trail," he said.

"And we helped them carry their backpacks down," Morgan added.

"That's good," a person said, "because when we saw them, we weren't sure they were going to make it down here."

"I wonder how they're going to hike out of here," Morgan said.

"I wonder how *we're* going to hike out of here," Dad said.

Morgan, James, and Dad put away their game. They gulped down the rest of their lemonade, then stepped outside and were blasted by the desert heat.

"Where's the air conditioning?" James joked.

"Or the ice machine!" Morgan added.

They turned on their flashlights and walked slowly back to the campground.

When they got to their campsite, they searched all around it. Then they opened the tent flap and quickly crawled inside.

Dad hurriedly zipped the tent up. Morgan, James, and Dad searched the corners and edges to make sure there were no critters inside.

Dad shone his flashlight on the tent zipper again to make sure it was completely closed.

They put sheets down on their mattress pads, took off their shoes, and lay down.

"No need for a sleeping bag tonight," Dad said.

They looked up through the mesh at the top of the tent and saw hundreds of stars.

"It's too hot to sleep," James said. He took his water bottle and squirted himself.

"Good idea," Dad said.

They lay silently, listening to the buzzing from the cicadas outside.

"What happens if we have to go to the bathroom?" James blurted out.

"We'll cross that bridge when we get there," Dad said.

"But whatever you do, don't go outside barefoot," Morgan reminded her brother.

Cicada

A while later, Morgan whispered, "James, are you asleep?"

"No," James replied, "are you?"

Morgan laughed. "It sounds like Dad's asleep."

"Does it?" Dad answered groggily. "Why do you say that?"

"I don't know," Morgan said. She laughed again. "What do you think?"

"Was I snoring?" Dad asked.

"Yes," James said. "But it's the heat that's keeping me awake."

"I wonder what time it is," Dad said.

"I'm not sure I want to know," Morgan replied.

Dad looked at his watch. "You're right, you don't want to know."

"Ahh!" Dad screamed. He kicked his feet around and sat up. He flicked on his flashlight and shone it on his feet, then frantically searched all around the tent.

Morgan and James also sat up.

"What's wrong, Dad?" Morgan asked.

"Something touched my leg!" Dad exclaimed.

"Do you want me to look?" James asked, grabbing his flashlight.

Most people who get stung by bark scorpions feel numbing and tingling near the sting. It can also become painful and hypersensitive to the touch. If someone is stung on the hand or foot, they might feel like electrical impulses are shooting up their limbs. These reactions usually peak in four to five hours.

But if the scorpion releases a lot of venom, the pain may spread to other limbs and throughout the body. The person may have vision problems and be unable to focus. It can also affect a person's breathing. People with these conditions need medical attention. Very young children, older people, and people with preexisting conditions are more likely to have serious problems when stung.

After being stung, it is best to dampen the area with a cold cloth, but not ice, and also take pain medication. Victims should also rest. Usually the pain goes away within twelve to twenty-four hours.

"No. Hold still," Dad replied. He slowly moved his leg out from under the sheet. "Ahh! It moved!" Dad flung his body to the side and landed on James's leg. James bumped into Morgan. The three scrunched together at the side of the tent.

"Were you stung?" Morgan asked.

"No," Dad answered.

Dad shone his flashlight on his sheet. Nothing was there.

"Maybe it crawled under it," Morgan said.

Dad slowly lifted the sheet and shone his light all around. Then he picked up a corner of the sheet and shook it.

A tiny crumpled leaf and a small twig fell to the floor of the tent.

Morgan and James looked at Dad. "Was that it?" Morgan asked.

Dad picked up the leaf and twig, unzipped the tent, and tossed them outside. "Maybe seeing all those scorpions earlier got me a bit skittish," Dad answered.

"I sure wouldn't want to be stung," James said.

Morgan, James, and Dad rearranged the tent.

"Hopefully we'll get some sleep now," Dad said while lying back down.

Sometime later, James opened his eyes. It was still dark outside. But he saw flashlights flickering about and he heard people moving around. "Are you guys up?" he whispered.

"It's not even five o'clock and people are packing," Dad answered. "I can't believe it."

"I guess there's only one way to beat the heat when you're camping at the bottom of the Grand Canyon," Morgan said.

"Should we get up?" James asked.

"We might as well," Morgan said. "We're not sleeping anyway."

"I don't know," Dad said. "We only have seven miles to hike today. We don't need to be in that much of a hurry."

James turned on his flashlight. He checked around the tent for scorpions and then found his park map. James studied the map. "We gain about 1,600 feet today."

There was a faint glow of morning light outside.

Morgan sat up. "I've got to go to the bathroom."

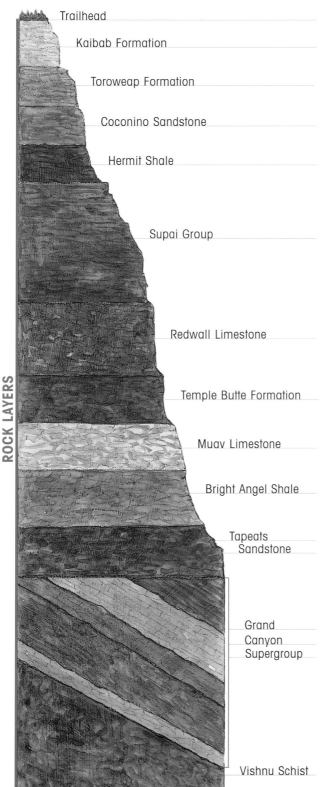

ROCK LAYERS

Trailhead

Kaibab Formation

Toroweap Formation

Coconino Sandstone

Hermit Shale

Supai Group

Redwall Limestone

Temple Butte Formation

Muav Limestone

Bright Angel Shale

Tapeats
Sandstone

Grand
Canyon
Supergroup

Vishnu Schist

"Me too," James said. James and Morgan picked up their shoes, turned them upside down, and shook them out.

Then they put on their shoes, opened the tent, and hurried to the bathroom.

When they got back to camp, they ate bagels and granola bars. Then Dad, James, and Morgan packed their tent. It was 6:30 a.m. when they were ready to go. They walked by Steve and Joanna's campsite.

"Steve and Joanna," Morgan whispered, "are you there?"

There was no answer.

"They're probably still asleep," Dad said. "I'm sure we'll see them on the trail."

Morgan, James, and Dad walked through Phantom Ranch. They passed the ranger quarters and the amphitheater where they had listened to the talk the night before. Then they walked by the canteen and dormitories. They stopped to fill their water bottles.

"Maybe we could stay in one of those stone cabins next time," Dad said.

"I don't know," James said, "I'm just as happy camping."

James, Morgan, and Dad got on the North Kaibab Trail.

"There are only fourteen miles and 6,000 feet of climbing to go!" James announced.

"That's all?" Morgan joked.

"Just think one step at a time," Dad said.

They hiked along Bright Angel Creek and quickly came into a narrow section of the canyon with cliffs rising hundreds of feet above them. Only a small part of the blue sky was visible.

James looked at the dark cliffs streaked with quartz on both sides of the trail. He checked his map. "They call this part of the canyon The Box," James said. "I guess it's because we're kind of boxed in. And the rock layer in here is called Vishnu Schist. It's the first of all the layers of rock we'll climb through on our way out of the canyon."

"BASEMENT" ROCKS

Vishnu Schist is one of the "basement" rocks in the Grand Canyon. That's because it is found at the bottom of the Grand Canyon. The basement rocks are made of gneisses (pronounced "nices") and schists with some areas of granite. The gneisses and schists are metamorphic rocks. They started out as other types of rock and were changed by heat and pressure through time to their current form. The granite is an igneous rock that is formed by heat from volcanic action. Vishnu Schist is estimated to be 1.68 to 1.84 billion years old. While these are old rocks, much older rocks are exposed elsewhere in the world—3-plus billion years in parts of Canada and 4-plus billion years in Australia.

"How many other rock layers are we going to hike through?" Morgan asked.

James looked at his map and started counting. "It looks like about twelve," James answered. "Vishnu Schist at the bottom is the oldest and Kaibab Limestone at the top is the newest, but it's still 270 million years old."

"We'll have to watch for these layers as we climb," Dad said.

Here is one way to remember the rock layers in the Grand Canyon from the top to near the bottom:

Know (Kaibab Formation),
The (Toroweap Formation),
Canyon's (Coconino Sandstone),
History (Hermit Shale),
Study (Supai Group),
Rocks (Redwall Limestone),
Made (Muav Limestone),
By (Bright Angel Shale),
Time (Tapeats Sandstone).

They hiked through The Box silently. It was pleasantly cool since the sun wasn't shining deep into the canyon yet. Birds chirped and the stream gurgled next to the trail.

Dad looked up. There were a few wispy clouds in the sky. "It's the best time of day to hike," he said. Dad got out his water and drank. "How far to the first water stop, James?"

"It's at Cottonwood," James answered. "I guess around five or six miles."

"Oops. I better save some then," Dad said.

After a while, they came upon an area full of large, tall grasses. The trail wove through the grassy area. The trail was muddy in spots, and it even had a few small puddles of water next to it.

"There must be a spring here," Morgan said.

"I'll say," Dad said. "Look at these, guys."

Morgan and James came over. Dad pointed out several tiny black frogs. They hopped away into the grass. "I guess where there's water, there's a home for wildlife," Dad said.

"I wonder what kind of frogs they are," Morgan said.

"I bet Mom would know," James said.

They hiked on.

While walking, Morgan looked up. "There's the rim we're going to."

Towering way above them in the distance was the top of the canyon. It was full of trees.

"That's a *long* way up there," Dad said.

"Hey, look at that bird!" James called out.

Far up in the sky a bird was drifting about. It flew slowly in circles. James got out the binoculars and watched the bird. "It looks like the one we saw yesterday."

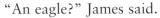

Morgan took a turn with the binoculars. "I think it has white patches under its wings."

Dad also looked. "I really want to know what kind of bird that is."

"An eagle?" James said.

"A hawk, maybe?" Morgan wondered.

"Or a condor?" Dad suggested. "I hope we find out."

A while later, they started climbing. Small pines and junipers were scattered about. A few cottonwood trees lined the creek along the trail. In the distance there was a small, cascading waterfall pouring off the canyon wall.

When they got closer, James checked his map. He noticed a short side trail. "That must be Ribbon Falls."

James took a long gulp of water.

"I wonder how long we'd last without water down here," Morgan said. She too took a good, long drink of water, then pulled an energy bar out of the side of her pack and started eating it.

The sun peeked over the cliff. Soon the whole trail was lit up with sunlight and the temperature immediately started to climb. They started sweating.

They hiked on over a few more rises and came to a ranger house nestled in a small grove of trees.

"This must be Cottonwood," James said.

The small campground was empty. They found a shady campsite on the left side of the trail and peeled off their packs.

"My back is soaked," Dad said.

"I can see that," James said. "What time is it?"

Dad looked at his watch. "It's eleven o'clock," he replied. "It's the perfect time to call it a day."

James, Morgan, and Dad set up camp. Once their tent was up, Dad crawled inside.

"I want to make sure the ground is level and comfortable," Dad announced.

"You're tired, aren't you?" Morgan asked.

"Yep," Dad replied.

Dad unrolled his Therm-a-Rest and then spread his sleeping bag out. He lay on top of the bag and called out, "It's comfortable!"

Morgan and James walked over to the tent. Dad had a hat pulled down over his eyes. "It's time for me to get some of the sleep I didn't get last night. How about you two? Are you tired?"

"A little," James admitted.

"Not really," Morgan said. "Aren't you hot in there?"

"Not yet," Dad replied. "But I'm going to leave the doors and windows open."

"We'll keep the scorpions out," James said.

Dad opened his eyes. "Promise?"

"And all the snakes too," Morgan added.

"With you two guarding me, I should be fine!" Dad said.

Morgan walked over to the shaded picnic table and sat down.

James got his backpack down from the pole. He loosened his small pillow from the straps and pulled it out. Then James got out the binoculars and walked back to the picnic table. He lay down on the bench and rested his head on the pillow.

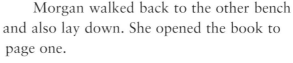

James looked up at the blue sky in between the trees. He searched the horizon and saw the canyon rim far above. He noticed a few small, puffy clouds in the sky. But otherwise, the sun was blaring down.

Morgan looked at James. She went to her backpack and got out her pillow. She found her book, *Brighty of the Grand Canyon* by Marguerite Henry. "I can't think of a better time to start reading this," she said to James.

Morgan walked back to the other bench and also lay down. She opened the book to page one.

A shaggy, young burro lay asleep in the gray dust of the canyon trail. Except for the slow heaving of his side and an occasional flick of an ear, he seemed part of the dust and ageless limestone that rose in great towering battlements behind him.

Morgan flicked a bug away and continued reading.

Several hours later, James was still lying on the picnic table bench. He was looking at the map of their hike for the next day. "We might have been able to climb out today," he thought to himself. Then he sat up. But the heat zapped his energy. James felt a bit dizzy. He guzzled down water, poured some on his head, then looked around. Morgan was on the other bench. She appeared to be asleep. James saw Dad's feet sticking out of the doorway of the tent. James scanned the sky again but didn't see anything. He got up and walked to the trail. James looked toward Phantom Ranch and saw shimmers of heat coming up from the bottom of the canyon. He walked back to the campsite.

"How hot do you think it is?" Morgan asked.

"I thought you were asleep," James said.

"I thought *you* were asleep," Morgan said.

"I bet it's almost 110 degrees," James answered. He went over to his pack, pulled out his journal, and wrote.

Thursday, August 4

This is James Parker reporting again. Here I am during the hottest part of the day in one of the hottest places in the world. We are at Cottonwood Campground, which, luckily, has some trees and shade. We are all resting. Dad is sleeping in the tent. And Morgan is reading. I don't see anything moving out here, and I can understand why.

I wonder what Mom's doing on the rim. Hopefully she's cooler than we are. Maybe she's up there reading a book or looking at the view. I wonder if she's looking out over the canyon to see if she can find us.

Anyway, yesterday we made it safely into the canyon and to Phantom Ranch. I wonder how we're going to do hiking out tomorrow. So far, the hike hasn't been too difficult. But it's all uphill from here. Will we be able to make it? I guess we'll find out.

Reporting from the Grand Canyon,

James Parker

James saw a bird flying in the air. It was so far up that it seemed like it was close to the rim. James grabbed the binoculars and moved them around until he spotted the bird. Then he followed it for a while.

The bird drifted around in circles. James noticed that the end of its wings splayed out like fingers. "I wonder if it's the same bird," James whispered. Then the bird disappeared over a cliff.

James lay back on the bench and closed his eyes.

Morgan placed the marker in her book and closed it. She had just finished another chapter of *Brighty of the Grand Canyon*. Brighty had fallen asleep in a cave and a mountain lion snuck up and attacked him. But Brighty fought off the lion and drowned him in a pool of water. Because of the fight, Brighty was hurt and couldn't walk.

She got up from the bench and walked out from under the trees. "I sure wouldn't want to run into a mountain lion down here," she said while looking around. Morgan walked back to camp. James was lying on the other bench and Dad was still in the tent. James's diary lay on the table. Morgan got up and went over to her pack and pulled out her own diary.

Dad heard her rustling about. "Is someone alive out there?"

Morgan laughed. "Yes. It's just me and a few scorpions!"

"Can you do me a favor, Morgan?" Dad asked. "Can you fill up my water bottles?"

"Sure," Morgan replied. She walked over to the tent. Dad sat up and handed her two empty water bottles.

"Thanks," Dad said.

Morgan noticed Dad's book on the tent floor. It was *Desert Solitaire* by Edward Abbey.

"What a perfect book to read on this hike," Morgan said.

"Yes, it does fit," Dad said.

Morgan walked over to the water spigot. She filled up Dad's water bottles and her own. She took a long drink and then filled her bottle again. Morgan trudged back to camp.

"Here you go, Dad," Morgan said.

Dad immediately guzzled down water. "You two doing okay out there?"

"We're doing what you're doing," Morgan replied.

"It's really too hot to do anything else, isn't it?" Dad asked.

"Yes," Morgan agreed. She walked back to the picnic table and opened her diary.

Thursday, August 4
Dear Diary,
I'm in a very unusual place: the bottom of the Grand Canyon. But it feels like we are at the bottom of the world. And it's too hot to do anything, so we're all just resting in the shade and waiting for the sun to go down.
Last night we camped at Phantom Ranch. It was like no place I've been to before. It's a small little lodge for tourists in the middle of nowhere. But it has a restaurant and cabins, and I even heard it used to have a swimming pool. We camped a short ways away in the campground next to a creek.

But the spooky thing about it was the scorpions. We went to a night walk with a ranger and saw a bunch of them! Dad freaked out thinking there were scorpions in the tent. He even said he thought about sleeping on top of the picnic table! James and I were worried too. To be honest, I didn't get up to go to the bathroom because I was afraid of being stung. I wonder what would happen if I was? Would I be able to hike out?

I love the Grand Canyon though! I've taken dozens of pictures of the scenery. Now that I'm hiking in it, I've found that it's much bigger than I imagined.

Anyway, I think I'll try and take a nap. Dad says we'll need all the rest we can get for the big climb out tomorrow.

Sincerely,

Morgan

A few hours later, the sun dropped behind a canyon wall. Cottonwood Campground was covered in shade. It quickly felt much cooler.

James sat up. He looked around and then took a long drink of water. "Morgan?" he whispered.

"I'm awake," Morgan said. "What's up?"

"Do you want to walk around?" James asked.

"Okay," Morgan replied. Morgan and James walked over to the tent. Dad was rolled over sideways and his eyes were closed. "You can go," he muttered. "Just don't go too far or for too long. I'm going to get up in a bit and start getting dinner ready."

Morgan and James walked back to the main trail. They headed downhill.

James stopped by a small rock. He rolled the rock away with his foot and looked.

"No scorpions there," Morgan said.

They wandered off the trail.

Morgan grabbed James's arm. "Look!" she called out.

A large black-and-white striped snake raced into the bushes and disappeared.

"That was cool!" James said.

There are many different types of snakes at the Grand Canyon, including several types of rattlesnakes. The Grand Canyon pink rattlesnake lives only at the Grand Canyon. The whip snake has black and white stripes. Other common snakes are the king snake and gopher snake.

James and Morgan continued exploring. Using their boots, they moved a few small rocks.

"Anything?" James asked.

"Not yet," Morgan answered. "I wonder if we'll see any pottery or arrowheads. Joanna did say Native Americans lived down here."

Morgan and James heard voices. They looked up. A couple of hikers were walking up the trail.

"Hello down there!" James called out.

"Hello up there!" one of the hikers called back.

When the two hikers got closer, James and Morgan recognized them. They ran back to the trail so they could be at camp to meet them. Dad was busy preparing dinner. "Perfect timing," he said.

"Guess who's coming up the trail?" James asked.

"Who?" Dad replied.

"Steve and Joanna!" Morgan answered.

"Really?" Dad said. "That's great, they're hiking again in the canyon. It will be nice to see them."

After saying hello, Steve and Joanna found an empty site and set up their camp.

Morgan, James, and Dad sat down for dinner.

"My specialty," Dad announced, "vegetarian chili with textured vegetable protein."

Morgan ate a spoonful. "It's spicy."

"I like it," James said.

Thunder rumbled in the canyon. Morgan, James, and Dad looked up.

"I hadn't even noticed the storm," Dad said.

James walked out from under the trees. He held out his hand and waited a few seconds. "It's starting to rain," he announced.

Morgan and Dad joined James.

Far above them, lightning flashed. Several seconds later, thunder rumbled.

James pointed up to the dark clouds. "I bet it's pouring at the top of the canyon."

"Right where Mom is camped," Morgan said.

"And this is right where we shouldn't be during a thunderstorm," Dad added. "Let's not stand out in the open like this."

They moved back to their campsite under the trees and watched the storm from there. "I hope this is safe enough," Dad said.

A few scattered drops of rain plopped down. The wind picked up and it cooled down a few degrees.

"I wonder why it's not pouring down here," James said.

Morgan, James, and Dad looked up at the clouds. Veils of rain fell below the clouds.

"The rain's not making it all the way to the ground," Dad answered. "The desert air is sucking the moisture out of the storm."

DESERT RAIN

Much of the Inner Grand Canyon is desert. Deserts receive less than ten inches of rain a year. Sometimes when it rains on the rim above, the rain evaporates on the way to the ground. This is called virga. On average, the North Rim gets thirty inches of precipitation a year. The South Rim averages fifteen inches. The Inner Canyon averages about eight inches.

"I think we'll sleep a lot better tonight," Morgan said, "now that it's cooled off."

"And hopefully there won't be any critters around," Dad added.

They cleaned up after dinner. Dad set a lantern on the table.

Just before dark, Steve and Joanna walked down from their campsite.

"How about some dessert?" Steve offered.

"Chocolate chip cookies!" Joanna added.

"Sounds good to me," Dad said.

Steve and Joanna sat down. They placed a plate of crumbled cookies in the middle of the table. "I guess two days in a backpack messed up our dessert," Steve said.

Joanna saw Morgan's book *Brighty of the Grand Canyon*. "You're reading a novel I read to my fifth grade class every year."

"You were a fifth grade teacher?" Morgan asked. "That's the grade James and I will be in next year."

"I thought you were about that age," Joanna said. "I retired from teaching a few years ago."

"Now instead of telling kids what do to, she's telling me what to do," Steve joked.

Joanna laughed.

Dad lit the lantern. He took part of a cookie and passed the plate around.

"You know, Brighty was named after the creek we've been hiking by," Morgan said. "And the book says Brighty actually made the trail we're climbing to the North Rim."

"Brighty climbed here?" James asked. "He was lucky, then, to see such a beautiful place."

"*Brighty of the Grand Canyon* is one of my favorite stories," Joanna said. "But I bet it was Native Americans who actually helped create this trail. Speaking of great stories, we heard an interesting one at a campfire talk. Do you want to hear it?"

Morgan, James, Dad, and Steve turned toward Joanna at the picnic table. The lantern on the table lit their faces. Insects fluttered around the light.

"It was in the 1970s, I think," Joanna started.

"1977 to be exact," Steve said.

"Okay, it was 1977," Joanna repeated, looking at her husband. "A man wanted to walk across the whole canyon in less than twenty-four hours. He hiked down, camped, and then got up to get to the river by two in the morning." Joanna paused for a second. "That already sounds like too much hiking to me."

"Now he had fourteen miles and 6,000 feet of climbing left that day," Steve said.

"Anyway," Joanna went on, "the first part of the climb was gradual and fairly easy—just like the part we've been on today. But the last five miles above Roaring Springs became very steep."

"I can't imagine doing this trek in one day. It is hard enough in three days!" Steve said. "Besides, taking your time is a good thing. Otherwise you miss the scenery and all the interesting parts of the canyon, like the geology."

Joanna continued, "About four miles from the summit, the man was getting extremely tired. He turned a corner on the trail and saw a big boulder. On top of the boulder were three little green men."

Morgan, James, and Dad looked intently at Joanna.

"They were calling the man's name, saying, 'Bob, come here, come here,'" Joanna went on.

"Were there really green creatures in the canyon?" James asked.

"Not really," Joanna answered. "But Bob did see them. Apparently, when you have severe heat exhaustion and you're getting close to death, you can start hallucinating. The man knew this was happening to him. He was very scared, thinking he was about to die. So he kept his head down and counted his steps on the trail to keep his mind focused. And more than 7,000 steps later, he made it to the top of the canyon."

"Wow, what a story," Dad said.

"And it's a true one," Steve added. "The person who experienced it was Ranger Bob. That was many years ago, and now he gives campfire talks at the Grand Canyon."

"Am I telling the story, or are you?" Joanna asked Steve.

Morgan and James laughed.

"Our parents do that all the time!" Morgan said. "They finish each other's sentences."

"Do we, now?" Dad asked.

Joanna smiled. "Well, Ranger Bob also said that years later he hiked into the canyon for eight grueling days. But when he hiked out on the last day, he started crying. He felt like he was leaving a good friend behind."

"It is so much different in the canyon than at the rim," Morgan said. "You would have no idea from up there what it is like down here."

"Thanks for taking us on this trail, Dad," James said.

"I knew you would like it," Dad said. "And you are right, the Inner Canyon has to be seen up close."

Everyone sat quietly for a moment. Crickets chirped in the distance.

"I wonder how we're going to feel tomorrow when we finish our hike," James said. "Will we miss it here just like Ranger Bob?"

By the time Steve and Joanna went back to their campsite, it was late. Morgan, James, and Dad crawled into their tent. They left the rain fly off. They lay on top of their sleeping bags and looked up. A few stars appeared between the clouds and the leaves of the trees.

"I can sure get used to this," Dad said. "Not having to work and just backpacking with you guys."

"Where do you want to go next summer?" Morgan asked.

"Another national park?" James suggested.

"There are so many great ones," Dad said. "We'll have to pull out a map and figure that out when we get back. But I really want to take you to Yellowstone—the world's first national park. And Mom's been mentioning Yosemite and how beautiful it is."

Morgan, James, and Dad listened to the noise of the crickets. They stared up at the stars. A gentle breeze wafted through the tent and . . .

Morgan sat up. She heard voices and the sound of clanging pots. It was already light out. She looked at Dad and James. They were still asleep. Morgan slowly crawled out of the tent. Her book was sitting on the table.

Morgan opened *Brighty of the Grand Canyon* to the next chapter. She remembered that Brighty had just fought off a mountain lion.

All the next day, Brighty lay in misery. He kept biting at his cuts, trying to quiet the throbbing, but the gashes only widened and the burning pain ran up his legs. He moaned tiredly, and from time to time sank into a half sleep. He was too weak to eat, and he would not go near the tainted pool to drink.

"You sure went through a lot," Morgan said, as if Brighty were standing beside her. Then she heard James and Dad moving about in the tent.

Morgan, James, and Dad ate some instant oatmeal with dried fruit. They stuffed energy bars and trail mix in the outside pouches of their backpacks. Then they packed up camp, filled their water bottles, and clambered back to the trail.

"Here we go!" Dad said.

"Seven miles until we meet Mom," Morgan added.

Dad, Morgan, and James walked briskly uphill. Morgan put on the earplugs to her MP3 player.

"What are you listening to?" asked James.

"The 'On the Trail' part of the *Grand Canyon Suite*," Morgan answered.

"Sounds about right," Dad said.

The higher up they went, the more pine trees there were.

"We're climbing out of the desert," Dad announced.

"It's a good thing we did all that hiking back home to get in shape," James observed. "I bet it's really helping us now."

"You have to be ready for a hike like this," Dad said.

Morgan walked ahead. "I'm getting into a rhythm," she said, "and this music is helping me." The sounds of clopping feet filled her ears, just like a bunch of mules were walking on the trail.

A while later, Dad stopped and peeled off his backpack. He leaned it against a rock. Morgan and James waited for him.

"You should see how soaked your back is," James said.

"I can feel it," Dad said. He took out a handkerchief and wiped his face. "Now I know how those mules felt the other day. Going up is a lot different from going down." He took a long drink of water and then poured some on his handkerchief and rubbed it on his face. "Much better!" he exclaimed. "You guys should drink too."

Morgan and James both took long drinks.

"The next water stop isn't too far," James said.

The family continued to trudge uphill until they ran into Steve and Joanna. They were sitting at a picnic table eating snacks.

"Welcome to our spot in the shade," Steve said.

"Do you mind if we join you?" Dad asked.

Joanna moved over. "Please, have a seat!"

WATER AND FOOD

Grand Canyon hikers lose about a half to one and a half quarts of water per hour of hiking. Some people can lose up to three quarts per hour. Hikers in the Grand Canyon should carry at least four quarts of water per person per day in the summer. If hikers don't feel like eating or drinking, they should rest until they do. But drinking too much water and not eating enough salty foods can also cause a hiker problems. A balance of water and food is very important.

Morgan, James, and Dad got some snacks and their water bottles and sat down.

"There's a house over there!" James exclaimed. "It looks like someone lives down here."

"I wonder who?" Dad said, then turned toward Steve and Joanna. "You must have gotten up early today."

WATER AND ART

For many years, the pumphouse keeper at Roaring Springs was a man named Bruce Aiken. His house was about a half mile below Roaring Springs, and he lived in the canyon for more than thirty years. He had a very important job—to make sure water was being pumped from Roaring Springs throughout the canyon. Although Bruce does not live in the canyon anymore, he is an artist whose paintings are on display in local galleries.

"Before sunrise," Steve answered. "We were trying to take advantage of the cooler weather. But that's gone now."

After a few minutes, James, Dad, and Morgan got up and put their backpacks on. They refilled their water bottles.

"We ought to get going now too," Joanna said. "But I'm sure we'll be at a much slower pace than you. Hopefully we'll see you farther up the trail."

The trail quickly became steep. Morgan, James, and Dad pressed on. It was eleven o'clock and already hot. The sky was mostly clear with a few billowing clouds overhead. Morgan, James, and Dad's brisk morning pace had slowed.

"How far to the next water stop?" Dad asked James.

"Not far," James said, feeling sweat dripping down his face. "Roaring Springs is only seven-tenths of a mile from that house."

They hiked on and hiked up.

"I wonder what Mom is doing now," James said. He stopped and put his hands on a rock next to the trail to brace himself.

Dad caught up with James and walked next to him.

"Mom's probably sitting under a tree and reading," Morgan said.

"Resting under a tree sounds good to me," Dad said. He shifted his pack around to make it more comfortable.

James took a deep breath and trudged on.

"Look, we're passing into another layer of rock," Dad said. "It's a greenish gray color."

James looked at his map. "It's probably Bright Angel Shale," he announced.

They climbed some more until they heard a cascading waterfall. The sound of the water got louder as they got closer to it.

"It must be Roaring Springs," Dad said.

"I wonder if this is where Brighty used to go to haul water up to the rim," Morgan said.

Dad, Morgan, and James climbed toward the springs. They came to a junction in the trail where a steep path led down to the water.

"Do you want to go down there?" Dad asked.

James stood still and blinked his eyes. He wobbled for a moment and then stepped back and put his hand out against the cliff.

"Are you okay?" Morgan asked James.

"I just got a bit dizzy for a second," James answered.

"Well, that answers that," Dad said. "We're going down there to rest."

Dad moved behind James. He grabbed his pack and helped hoist it off his back. They took their water bottles and a few snacks. Then they propped their packs against the cliff and walked down to Roaring Springs.

WATER TO THE RIM

Starting in 1928, the Union Pacific Railroad pumped water up from Roaring Springs to the North Rim. Then in the 1960s, the transcanyon pipeline was built. This took water from Roaring Springs and pumped some up to the North Rim. A larger amount of water flows by gravity down the pipeline to Phantom Ranch and up the other side to Indian Garden. Several pumps at Indian Garden push the water up to the South Rim. Now all of the water for the Grand Canyon comes from Roaring Springs.

After resting a while in the shade, James stood up. "I'm so dirty, I can't believe it," he observed. Then he said, "I think we should get going now."

Morgan, James, and Dad climbed back to the main trail.

James grabbed his pack and stepped backward. His head felt like it was swaying back and forth. "The canyon is spinning," James thought. He put his head down for a few seconds and then stood back up. "Okay, I'm ready to go," he announced to Dad and Morgan.

Morgan, James, and Dad slowly lifted their packs and put them on. They left Roaring Springs behind.

As he walked uphill, James wondered if he was getting as tired as Steve and Joanna were the other day. He wanted to stop, but he was afraid that if he did, he wouldn't be able to get going again. If that happened, they would be late meeting Mom. The only thing to do was to go up, one step at a time. He started counting the steps in his head. "One . . . two . . . three . . . four . . ."

"I'm so glad you two came with me on this hike," Dad said, putting his hand on James's shoulder. "This is the best scenery in the world, and I wouldn't want to share this experience with anyone else."

James continued counting his steps. "Five . . . six . . . seven . . ."

At one of our rests

Dad stopped and looked up at the sky. "It's getting cloudy."

"Shade would be nice," James said.

"There are people way up there on the trail," Morgan noticed.

"That's a long ways up there," James said. "And they don't even have packs on."

"They must be day hikers coming down from the North Rim," Dad said.

James walked slowly. "It's getting hard to lift my legs," he said, then stopped and dropped his head down. James shook his head and started walking again.

Dad watched James. "Why don't we sit for a few minutes," he suggested.

What a trail!

They found a small overhanging rock that had just enough shade underneath it for the three of them. James peeled off his pack and let it drop to the ground. Morgan picked James's pack up and leaned it against a rock. She handed him his water bottle.

James drank some water and shook his head. "Now I know how Steve and Joanna felt the other day. I don't know how much farther I can go on."

"There's no hurry, James," Dad said.

"But we said we'd be at the trailhead before eight o'clock," James said.

"We still have plenty of time to get there, but if we're late, we're late," Dad said. "What's most important is how you are feeling."

Dad took out some pretzels and passed them to Morgan. She grabbed a few and handed the bag to James.

James leaned forward and put his elbows on his knees. "I'm not hungry."

"You need to eat," Dad said.

James grabbed a few pretzels. "I'll try," he said, putting one in his mouth.

While they were resting, Dad took the binoculars and searched the skies. He looked toward the rim and saw the forest above. "I bet it's at least ten degrees cooler up there," he said. Then he looked at the large clouds overhead. "Hmm, it looks like a storm is coming."

"Can I look?" Morgan asked.

Dad passed her the binoculars.

Morgan searched all around. While scanning the canyon, she saw a bird perched on a rock. It was gnawing on something.

"You guys have to see this!" Morgan exclaimed.

Morgan handed Dad the binoculars. He found the bird.

Suddenly the bird flapped its wings and took off. Dad watched the bird rise into the air. "I think it has a number under its wing," Dad said.

"A number?" James asked.

"I think," Dad answered. "I only had a glimpse."

The bird rose higher into the sky.

"Hmm, that's interesting," Dad said.

Thunder rumbled far off in the distance.

James sat up. "We better get going."

"Are you sure you're ready?" Dad asked.

"I don't know," James answered, "but I want to try."

"We don't have to hurry," Morgan said.

"Yes, we do," James said. "We'll be late for Mom."

Morgan helped James put on his backpack. James trudged uphill, and Dad and Morgan followed. They crossed a small bridge over a dry creek bed.

More thunder rumbled.

"I think," James said, as he took a step and then another, "I think . . ." He took yet another step and put his hand and forehead against the cliff.

Dad and Morgan stopped and watched James. James continued walking uphill.

They hiked up the steep switchbacks, heading toward Supai Tunnel.

"I think I'm getting really tired," James finally said.

Again, thunder rumbled from far away.

"Can you go on?" Morgan asked.

"I don't know," James said. "I'll try." He drank more water.

Dad pulled a granola bar out of his pack and handed it to James.

James took a bite. "Thanks, Dad."

They hiked on. Farther up the trail, the switchbacks became shorter and steeper. James stopped again and leaned back against a rock wall. He closed his eyes. Morgan stopped and leaned over.

Dad took a deep breath and looked down at the bridge far below. "We've climbed a long way," he said. "Good job, both of you. That was tough climbing."

"This is the hardest part by far," Morgan said.

"How are you doing now, James?" Dad asked.

"I don't know," James answered while putting his arm against the cliff and steadying himself. He took a deep breath and took a step up the trail. James slowly took another step. Then another, and another.

Thunder rumbled again. Drops of rain plunked down.

The trail led into a short tunnel.

They walked through it.

"Look, a water fountain!" Morgan called out.

James looked up at the water spigot. Suddenly he dropped his pack onto the ground, rushed over to the bushes, and threw up.

James closed his eyes. "Ohh!" he moaned. "I feel awful."

Morgan walked over to her brother and put a cool, wet bandanna on his forehead. She soaked the bandanna in water again and wiped off his face.

James leaned back against a rock. "Do you mind if we sit here a while?"

Dad put his hand on James's back. "You rest as long as you need to."

A half hour later, James was still in the same spot.

"Do you want us to get help?" Dad asked.

"No, just let me rest a while longer," James replied.

The sky flashed with lightning. Thunder shook the canyon.

James sat up. "That was close."

Then the storm let loose. Sheets of rain poured down. James, Morgan, and Dad watched the rain for a moment, enjoying the cool relief it brought.

"I'm getting soaked!" Dad yelled above the sound of the storm.

"We can go in there!" Morgan shouted, pointing to the tunnel.

Dad helped James up and walked with him into Supai Tunnel.

Morgan grabbed James's backpack and ran with it into the tunnel. Then she went back outside and got the other packs.

The rain poured down even harder.

James, Morgan, and Dad sat next to each other and watched it rain.

"I guess Grofé really knew what a day in the Grand Canyon was like when he wrote the *Grand Canyon Suite*," Morgan said.

James started nibbling on a cracker.

"There you go," Dad said. "You'll have your appetite back in no time."

James took another bite of the cracker.

Morgan watched the large drops of rain splash onto the muddy trail. A tiny stream of water formed on the trail and trickled downhill. Morgan pulled out her journal.

Friday, August 5
Dear Diary,

It's pouring rain outside, and we can't hike right now. We're waiting in Supai Tunnel. We needed to take a break anyway because James is sick.

This trip has been a real test of our strength. It's a hard trail! We've been climbing for what seems like forever, and we're getting close to the top, we think.

But really, I like all this. We've seen scorpions, different rock layers, desert plants, and this unusual bird with a number clipped on its wing. Anyway, I hope we can make it to the top of the canyon today. I can't wait to see Mom and get a hot shower and into some clean clothes.

Yours,
Morgan

Rain continued to come down in sheets. Thunder boomed again.

"I think I'm feeling better," James announced. He stood up quickly, but immediately sat back down and dropped his face into his hands. "But maybe not completely better."

"You're not seeing anything that's not real, are you?" Morgan asked seriously.

James paused a second then looked at Morgan. His lips curled up. "Not unless my messy haired, filthy dirty, soaking wet twin sister is all in my imagination," he answered. "But, no. I haven't seen any little green munchkins."

Morgan grinned. "You *are* getting better."

"I feel good enough to write in my journal," James said.

Morgan pulled James's diary out of his pack.

"Can you get my map too?" James asked.

Morgan handed the map, journal, and a pen to James.

James opened his journal and spread the map out so he could see everything.

"You look like a reporter there with all your notes," Dad said.

James smiled and then started writing.

Friday, August 5

This is James Parker reporting,

I'm hiding out from a rainstorm in Supai Tunnel on the North Kaibab Trail in the Grand Canyon. We've covered nearly twenty miles on our journey, and we have 1.7 miles and 1,500 feet of elevation gain left. But at the moment, we don't know when we'll get to the top. I barfed a while ago, and I don't even have the flu! I keep getting dizzy when I get up and . . .

They heard footsteps sloshing up the trail.

A woman wearing ranger gear walked into the tunnel. "It's really coming down out there," she said.

Two more hikers also walked in. "Steve and Joanna," Morgan greeted them, "you made it!"

"The rain has really cooled things off," Steve said. "We're actually doing quite well today."

"Not me," James said, "I've been sick the last few hours."

The ranger stepped up to James. "I'm Angie," she introduced herself. "I'm a PSAR ranger, which stands for Preventive Search and Rescue. It sounds like I'm in the right spot."

Angie asked James some questions. Then she took his pulse. "Now will you stand up?" she asked James. Then she took his pulse again. She shone a small flashlight in James's eyes to check his pupils. She used a stethoscope to listen to his breathing.

While Angie checked James, she explained, "We're out here daily, patrolling the trails and making sure everyone has enough food and water. There are lots of heat problems in the canyon—although I imagine less so today, with the weather like this."

"I think James has heat exhaustion," Angie concluded. "You are lucky it hasn't gotten too extreme and become heatstroke. That would be very dangerous. Unfortunately, heat issues are very common in the Grand Canyon. That's why we have PSAR people out here. But the best thing for you right now, James, is to rest, eat, drink water, and cool down."

"You're like a portable doctor on the trail," Morgan said.

"Well, not quite," Angie said, "but we do what we can. Do you think you could walk around now?" she asked James.

"I think so," James answered. James walked back and forth in the tunnel.

"How does that feel?" Angie asked.

"Better," James answered.

"Do any of you need food or water?" Angie asked.

"We have plenty of food," Dad answered.

"And there's a water faucet right outside," Morgan added.

"Do you think you'll be able to hike out?" Angie asked James.

"I think so," he replied. "If I rest a bit more. It's not that far."

Thunder rumbled again. Rain continued to pour down.

"Well, it's not like we're able to go anywhere right now," Dad said.

"Good point," Angie said. "And the weather is certainly cooling down. That's half the battle right there."

James walked with Angie over to the opening of the tunnel. "We have to wait for the rain to stop before going on anyway," said James.

Angie looked back at the group. "I'm going to head out now to check on other hikers. Just take your time climbing up. With all the rain, the trail may be slippery in spots. Do you have flashlights?"

"We've got three," Morgan answered.

"We've got one too," Joanna replied.

"It's sure great to know there are people like you out here checking up on us," James said.

"I guess that's all part of visiting the Grand Canyon," Dad added.

James swung his backpack onto his back and walked out of Supai Tunnel. Dad high-fived James as he walked by.

Morgan, Dad, Steve, and Joanna followed James onto the trail. They continued their climb uphill.

Mom sat in the car at the North Kaibab Trail parking lot. It was 7:45 p.m. She flipped on her windshield wipers. A few drops of rain hit the car window. "The storm seems to be ending," she thought.

Mom got out of the car. It was surprisingly cool. She grabbed a windbreaker and walked across the parking lot to the trailhead. She looked down the empty trail and waited a few minutes. "James! Morgan! Robert!" she called out. But there was no answer. Mom paced back and forth, stopping often to look down the trail. By the time she got back to the car, it was 8 p.m.

James, Morgan, Dad, Steve, and Joanna trudged up the trail. It was nearly dark, and Morgan led the way with her flashlight. The edge of the trail dropped off and plunged straight into the canyon.

"I wonder how far down you'd fall," James said, peering over the edge.

"Let's not find out," Dad said. "Please stay away from the cliff."

James moved back to the center of the trail.

Steve started singing.

Show me the way to go home
I'm tired and I want to go to bed

I got sick about an hour ago
And it went straight to my head

James laughed and they all joined in.

Show me the way to go home
I'm tired and I want to go to bed . . .

Mom got out of the car again. It was 8:30 p.m. and completely dark. She grabbed a flashlight and walked to the trailhead. Mom started walking down the North Kaibab Trail. The trail was thick with mud in spots. Mom watched her step to make sure she didn't slip. Lightning flickered in the distance, but she heard no thunder.

Mom continued walking. After a while, she reached a large, flat rock next to the trail. Mom stepped out onto the rock and looked out over the canyon. It was pitch black.

"Where are they?" Mom wondered.

"Hello . . . down . . . there!" Mom called out.

"Hello . . . down . . . there!" the black canyon answered back.

"Hello!" Mom called out once more, and again the canyon echoed back.

Mom stood at the lookout for a moment longer. "Maybe I should go back up and tell the rangers three hikers are missing," she thought.

A tiny flickering light appeared somewhere in the canyon. Mom waved her flashlight back and forth and turned it off and on. She saw the light again. Then it was gone.

Morgan and the others hiked on. All they heard were the sounds of their footsteps tromping up the trail.

"Wait a second!" Morgan said. She stopped the group. "I thought I saw a light."

Everyone stood still for a moment and looked up the canyon.

"I guess not," Morgan said.

They hiked on.

A while later, Morgan froze again. "Wait. Listen."

They heard a voice yell, "Hello!" It echoed throughout the canyon.
"Hello!" Morgan called back.

"Hello!" the voice called again.

"That voice sounded familiar," Dad said. "Come on!"

Morgan led the group quickly up several more switchbacks. She
turned a bend in the trail. A light up ahead moved back and forth.
Morgan walked briskly toward the light.

"Maybe it's the light at the end of the tunnel!" James exclaimed.

They hiked faster up a flatter part of the trail.

When Morgan got closer to the light, she shielded her eyes and said,
"Hello?"

James, Dad, Steve, and Joanna caught up.

"Who's there?" Morgan
said as she walked even
closer.

"Who do you think?"
the voice behind the light said.

"Mom!" Morgan called
out. She dropped her flashlight
and ran up and hugged her
mother.

"Mom!" James called out.

"Honey!" Dad said. He
walked over and kissed Mom.

"Sorry we're late, Mom,"
James said. "But I got sick and had to
rest."

"And then a storm came and we
hid out in a tunnel," Morgan added.

"A rescue ranger found us in the
tunnel and checked on James," Dad said.

"Steve and Joanna were with her,"
Morgan added.

Joanna stepped forward. "James finished the hike all on his own."

"We all did," James corrected. "And now we're finally at the top!"

"The top?" Mom responded. "Well, not exactly. I think we're at Coconino Point. We're still about three-fourths of a mile from the top. I came down the trail looking for you."

"You mean we have more climbing to do?" Steve asked.

"Just a little," Mom replied.

"Come on," Dad said. "Hot showers, food, and soft mattress pads await above. Let's go!"

They marched on.

"Follow the red, muddy trail," Dad said in a high-pitched voice. "Follow the red, muddy trail," he repeated in as low of a voice as he could.

"Follow the red, muddy trail," Morgan said while holding her nose.

James laughed. "We're not in Oz!"

"Follow the red, muddy trail," Steve squeaked.

"Follow the red, muddy trail," Joanna added.

They started singing as they pranced up the trail.

"Follow, follow, follow, follow, follow the red, muddy trail!"

"Because, because, because, because, because! Because of the wonderful things it does!"

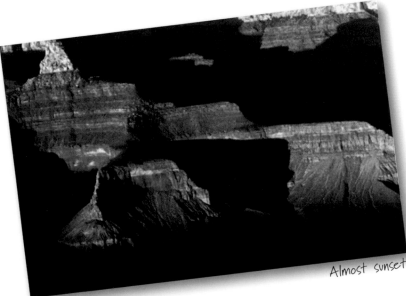

Almost sunset

Morgan yawned and stretched.

She looked around the room at the Grand Canyon Lodge. Other visitors were also sitting on couches and chairs, resting, talking, reading, and looking out at the view.

Morgan got up from the couch and shuffled over to the window. "My legs are so sore," she said to herself.

Morgan stared out at the Grand Canyon. Far across it, on the South Rim, she saw a trail leading down. "I can't believe we crossed all that," she thought.

Morgan looked at the sheer cliffs and colorful buttes throughout the canyon. The mesas on top of the canyon were bathed in sunlight. The lower canyon was darkened by shadows. In the hazy distance, several sharp mountain peaks rose high in the sky.

"I can see why this is the 'canyon that all canyons are compared to,'" she said. "It is grand."

Morgan looked out. There were large clouds towering high in the sky. "I wonder if we're going to get another thunderstorm today," she thought. "Well, if we do, it would sure be nicer to experience it from the lodge."

Morgan turned around and saw her family. Dad was asleep with his head draped over an arm of the couch. James was also asleep, leaning against Mom. Mom was sketching. Morgan shuffled back to join them.

"You're walking a little slowly," Mom said. "Are you okay?"

"I can barely lift my legs," Morgan answered.

A World Heritage Site is considered one of the world's most scenic or cultur-ally significant places. According to the United Nations Educational, Scientific, and Cultural Organization (UNESCO), in order to be considered a World Heritage Site, a national park should be the following:

1. An outstanding example of the Earth's evolutionary processes
2. An outstanding example of geologic processes, biological evolution, and human interaction with the natural environment
3. A place containing outstanding natural features, including forma-tions, ecosystems, and beauty
4. A place containing significant habitats for threatened species of animals

In 1979, it was decided that the Grand Canyon met the above criteria and it was labeled a World Heritage Site. The Grand Canyon is one of twelve natural World Heritage Sites in the United States. Some of the others include Yosemite National Park in California, Florida's Everglades, Hawaii Volcanoes National Park, Great Smoky Mountains in North Carolina and Tennessee, Kentucky's Mammoth Caves, New Mexico's Carlsbad Caverns, Wash-ington's Olympic National Park, Montana's Glacier National Park, and Yellowstone in Wyoming, Idaho, and Montana.

"I can only imagine how tough that hike was," Mom said. "How's the view?"

"Awesome," Morgan replied. "Especially now that I've crossed it and know what it looks like up close."

"It sure makes you proud when you accomplish something like that, doesn't it?" Mom asked.

I feel pretty good about it," Morgan answered. "What are you drawing?"

"Just something I started the other day after my art class," Mom explained. "I was drawing the whole canyon, but then I got interested in the little things. This picture is of a deer I saw at our campground one morning when you were gone."

"Can I see?" Morgan asked.

Mom moved the sketch pad so Morgan couldn't see it. "Maybe soon. By the way, do you remember seeing a house in the canyon?"

"Yes, we stopped and ate a snack there," Morgan answered. "It was on our way up."

"Well, the person who taught my class is an artist named Bruce Aiken. He used to live down there."

"Really?" Morgan said. "It's a small world, isn't it?" Morgan looked back at the statue of Brighty.

Mom looked at Morgan. "You know, I read something about that statue. It said that if you touch Brighty's nose, he'll bring you good luck."

"He will?" Morgan asked. She walked over to Brighty's statue and rubbed her hand on his nose. "I remember bumping into the statue before our hike," she thought. "And we did have good luck. We got back safely."

A BURRO NAMED BRIGHTY

Miners introduced burros into the canyon to help carry supplies. But when the Grand Canyon was turned into a national park in 1919, most mining ended, and all burros were either set free or escaped.

Wild burros caused problems in the Grand Canyon. They ate native plants and polluted water holes. By 1981, the burros were either killed or removed from the park and taken to adoption centers.

Brighty, nicknamed "the Hermit of Bright Angel Creek," was one of these burros. He lived at the Grand Canyon from around 1892 until 1922, and he regularly visited the North Rim each morning for pancakes. Brighty was friendly toward humans and was captured and put to work hauling water and supplies. Brighty was especially friendly to children. He gave boys and girls rides on his back. In 1953, Marguerite Henry wrote the famous children's book *Brighty of the Grand Canyon.*

Morgan walked back over to her family. She pulled out her journal, glanced up once more at Brighty, and started writing.

Saturday, August 6
Dear Diary,

I'm sitting here looking at the statue of Brighty, and I've been reading the book about him too! I wish I could have been here to see the real Brighty. It would have been neat to have a companion like him while hiking to keep us company and help haul our supplies. Maybe I could have even gotten a ride from him!

It's our last full day at the park and I'm hanging out at the Grand Canyon Lodge with my family. We are all resting after our rim-to-rim hike across the Grand Canyon. Dad said crossing the canyon was the most difficult thing he's ever done in his life. I remember my feet feeling like they were on fire. And when we got done, I don't think I've ever been so dirty in my whole life. But it was worth it. And I would do it again.

Anyway, James is waking up now. And even though we didn't want to do anything today, there's a talk outside on the patio that he and I want to go to.

Yours,
Morgan

James elbowed Dad. "It's past two o'clock," he whispered.

"Huh?" Dad mumbled. He sat up, opened his eyes, and looked at James. Then he looked at Morgan, who was standing beside him. "Boy, you two sure have recovered quickly!" Dad sat back. "But I don't know if I have. Go ahead without me."

"I'd like to go," Mom said.

Mom, James, and Morgan walked outside and joined other visitors. When they got there, the ranger was already talking. "Condors had lived in Arizona for 50,000 years. But starting in the early 1900s, condors no longer had the right food supply. Also, some eggs were stolen, condors collided with power lines, some had lead poisoning, and others ate antifreeze from cars. By 1982, there were only twenty-two condors left in the wild, all in California."

"How sad," Morgan commented.

The ranger continued. "A few years later, the remaining wild condors were captured and bred in captivity. They were later released in central California and northern Arizona. Today, condors are a regular sight here at the canyon."

"Do you think that's the type of bird we saw?" Morgan asked James.

"Could be," James said. "That's what Dad was thinking."

"If you saw one of those," Mom said, "you were very lucky."

The ranger went on. "Condors are scavengers. They finish off eating what other animals have started. And they can live up to sixty years! Condors are amazing to see because they're so rare. Now I'll need a couple of volunteers to help me."

Several hands went up. The ranger pointed to James and Morgan. "How about you two?"

James and Morgan walked up to the ranger.

"Thanks for helping me," the ranger said. "Can you tell us your names?"

"I'm James."

"And I'm Morgan."

"It's hard to imagine a condor's incredible size," the ranger explained. "So Morgan and James will help show us."

The ranger handed Morgan one end of a long roll of black felt. She gave the other end to James. "Walk apart," the ranger instructed.

Morgan and James walked away from each other and held up the felt until it was fully stretched out. It was cut into the shape of a large bird's wings.

"That's more than nine feet long!" the ranger said.

James looked at Morgan and then at the wings. He turned to the ranger. "We saw a bird that had wings just like this."

"And it had a number on it," Morgan added.

"You definitely saw a condor," the ranger said. "Lucky you! Those numbers help us keep track of them. We tracked one condor with a radio tag. It traveled 500 miles in two days."

A person in the audience suddenly looked up. "A condor!" she called out.

Several large birds were circling over the canyon. People grabbed their cameras and binoculars.

"They have white patches under their wings," one person said.

"The end of their wings are splayed," another person added.

The audience watched the birds circle around in the sky.

After the talk, James and Morgan ran back into the lodge where Dad was.

"Guess what?" James said.

Dad looked up from his reading. "What?"

"We know what kind of bird it was!" Morgan exclaimed.

"The one from the canyon?" Dad asked.

"Yeah," James said. "The talk on the patio was all about it."

James filled Dad in on condors.

"You were right," Morgan said.

"Interesting," Dad said. "It's great to know that condors are living around here."

"And," Morgan continued, "there's another talk about geology at four o'clock. Can we go?"

"Boy, you two are really interested in the Grand Canyon now," Mom said. "That's great!"

"I think once you've crossed it and seen so much of it," James explained, "you really want to learn more."

"I'm interested in that talk too," Dad said. "I should be able to move again by then."

At 4 p.m., the ranger trotted up to the patio outside the lodge with a box of supplies. "Welcome to the North Rim of the Grand Canyon," she said. "My name is Pam. Usually we do this geology talk right here on the patio. But today we're going to make a change. The talk will be inside the lodge because there's a chance of thunderstorms. Come on, everybody." The ranger opened the door and guided the group inside.

As soon as they all were in the lodge, it started raining. James, Morgan, Mom, and Dad sat on one of the lodge couches. Streaks of lightning flashed through the sky, followed by booming bursts of thunder.

"If you're like me, you'll want to watch this storm," Pam said to the group. "And here at the Grand Canyon, our weather sure puts on a show, as you can see."

Hail started pelting against the lodge windows. James and Morgan stood up and watched the tiny, icy balls bounce like marbles off the concrete patio.

"It's just like the 'Cloudburst' section in the *Grand Canyon Suite*," Morgan said. "I can almost hear the music."

Lightning ripped across the sky. Thunder cracked and shook the lodge. James and Morgan ran back to their parents.

"That was close," James announced.

The storm raged on. Dad, Mom, James, and Morgan huddled together.

"I'd sure rather be in here than out there," Dad said.

Once the storm calmed down, Pam showed the visitors some rocks she had from the canyon's different layers. She talked about the dates of the rocks in the canyon.

"And," Pam mentioned at the end of her talk, "the lodge here is built on the top layer, the Kaibab Formation. We've found fossils or fossilized tracks of sponges, worms, shells, corals, and brachiopods, which are like clams, in this layer. These fossils are about 270 million years old."

James raised his hand. "Why are there fossils of ocean animals at the Grand Canyon?"

"Good question," Pam said. "The Kaibab Formation was formed under the ocean before the whole area lifted up millions of years ago. If you get a chance tomorrow, hike out to Bright Angel Point and look for these types of fossils. There are many of them in the rocks next to the trail. Or, come back to our geology talk at four o'clock and I'll take you there!"

When Pam left, the family watched the rest of the storm from inside the lodge. Lightning continued to flash, but the thunder wasn't as loud. After a while, the thunderstorm ended and rays of sun peeked through the clouds.

James got up and walked to the viewing window. "It's not raining anymore," he announced. "Do you want to go out and look for those fossils?"

Mom looked at Morgan and Dad. "Sure!" she replied.

They put on their sweatshirts and walked outside.

Morgan, James, Mom, and Dad headed toward Bright Angel Point. Steam rose off the ground. There were small piles of hail next to the trail. The sky along the horizon was pink and orange.

"Look at the canyon!" Mom exclaimed. "It's full of shadows from the clouds."

"Look at the side of the trail," James said. "It looks like it just snowed."

Suddenly a bright shaft of light streamed through a dark gray cloud. The sunlight lit up a mesa in the distance. The family stopped to look.

"What a beautiful sight," Dad said.

"We're finally getting to see our Grand Canyon sunset," Morgan added. She pulled out her camera. "Time for pictures!"

"Ahh, sweet sunshine!" a man next to them said.

James looked over at the man. "Hey, it's the bike rider!"

The man turned toward the family. "I remember you, you're the family from Cape Royal Road. How was your trip across the canyon?"

"Great!" Morgan said. "I really recommend it. Hey, can you take our picture?"

"Sure," the man said.

Morgan, James, Mom, and Dad stood with their arms around each other.

The man looked at the viewing screen on the back of the camera. "Ready?" He snapped the picture and then gave the camera back to Morgan.

"Thanks," she said.

"Look, there's a rainbow!" Morgan called out.

The family looked across the canyon. In the eastern sky was a slowly fading rainbow. Toward the west, the brilliantly glowing sun slipped down to the horizon. The jagged outlines of the many cliffs and mesas were silhouetted against the hazy evening sky.

Morgan snapped several pictures.

"It looks like a painting," Mom commented.

The sun dropped out of sight, instantly turning the canyon walls a deep gray.

"There it goes," James said.

SUNRISE, SUNSET

There is no place on Earth that is better for watching the sunrise and sunset than the Grand Canyon.

Sunrise and sunset times are listed in current park newspapers. It is a good idea to arrive at viewpoints before sunrise or sunset. This gives visitors a chance to enjoy the moment as it unfolds and the changing colors in the canyon.

A MUST-SEE

Hopi Point on the South Rim is the most popular spot for watching the sunset. But many other canyon viewpoints are considered equally spectacular and are often less crowded.

As geologist Clarence Dutton once said about a Grand Canyon sunset, "The colossal buttes expand in every dimension." As the sun lowers, some people see colors changing in the sky, shadows and shapes shifting in the canyon, shafts of sunlight poking through clouds, and sometimes even a rainbow. Whatever the experience, a sunrise or sunset is a must-see while visiting the Grand Canyon.

The family watched the sky slowly turn darker. They stood for a few moments until the canyon could no longer be seen. The first stars appeared in the sky.

"How about some hot chocolate?" Dad suggested. "I think the cafe is open."

"Sure!" James answered.

The family walked back up to the lodge and out the front entrance. They walked into the cafe and ordered their drinks. Once they sat down, Mom pulled out a piece of paper.

"Now that you've hiked it, I want to know what you think of an early explorer's opinion of the Grand Canyon," Mom said. "I heard this at a campfire talk while you were gone. It was written by Joseph Ives, one of the first white people to ever see the canyon."

The region last explored is, of course, altogether valueless. It can be approached from the south, and after entering it there is nothing to do but to leave. Ours has been the first, and doubtless the last, party of explorers to visit this profitless locality. It seems intended by nature that the Colorado River, along the greater portion of its lonely and majestic way, shall be forever unvisited and undisturbed.

Mom stopped reading and looked at her family. "So, what do you think?"

"Boy, was he wrong," Dad said.

"I agree," Morgan added. "I know I'll come here again."

"I feel like I've just begun to explore here," James added.

Mom tore up the note and dropped it into her empty hot chocolate cup. "I thought you would feel that way," she said. "In the class I took, we learned that many artists, painters, and writers have been inspired by this place."

"Like Grofé, who wrote the *Grand Canyon Suite*," Morgan said.

"Speaking of writers," James said, "is there time for me to write in my journal?"

"Sure," Dad said.

James got his journal out of his pack and started writing.

Saturday, August 6

Dear Diary,

This is James Parker reporting. Tomorrow we are heading home from our adventure in the Grand Canyon. I feel like a real explorer now. And I feel like I want to keep doing trips like this. Morgan and I are already hounding our parents about where we're going to go next summer. And even though I got sick, I definitely want to go backpacking in the Grand Canyon again someday. Here is a list of my favorite places in the park:

1. Grand Canyon Lodge on the North Rim
2. Cape Final
3. Angel's Window
4. Roaring Springs
5. Phantom Ranch
6. Desert View Tower
7. Ooh-Ahh Point
8. Ribbon Falls
9. Bright Angel Point
10. The North Rim Campground

Anyway, it's sad leaving this place. But my parents said, "We can always come back!"

Yours until next summer,

James

While James wrote, Morgan also pulled out her journal. "I guess I have a few more things to write," she said.

Saturday, August 6
Dear Diary,
James and I are sitting here writing in our diaries about our incredible trip to the Grand Canyon. I see that he just wrote his top ten list. I agree with his list but think the Cliff Spring Trail and Point Imperial should also be on it. It was neat to see how Native Americans lived in the area at Cliff Spring. And Point Imperial was really an amazing view! I guess it's hard to come up with just ten places for my list.

Joanna used to teach fifth grade. She said she's going to send James and me some stuff from her classroom like books and magazines. I can't wait to get them! And I can't wait to finish Brighty, which, hopefully, I'll do in a few days. Joanna also gave us her e-mail address, so now I have a pen pal, in case I need help with my homework or if I want to remember the great times we had here in the park.

And, guess what? It rained again today. It kind of makes me sad. Now whenever there is a thunderstorm, it will make me think of the Grand Canyon. And I'll wish I was back here.

But I can always listen to the Grand Canyon Suite to help remind me of this place!
Sincerely,
Morgan

Morgan closed her diary.

James put his pen down. "Okay," he said. "I'm all done." He took out his flashlight. "Follow me."

James guided his family past the lodge and onto the Transept Trail heading toward the campground.

"At least it will be nice and cool tonight," Dad said. "It's great sleeping weather."

"And we're camped in the forest," Morgan added. "Scorpion free!"

"Added bonus!" James called back. "And there are showers nearby!"

"Life's just perfect, isn't it?" Mom said.